OVER HERE

OVER HERE

Alan Hunter

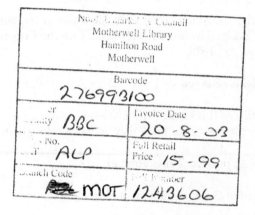
Chivers
Bath, England
•
Thorndike Press
Waterville, Maine USA

This Large Print edition is published by BBC Audiobooks Ltd, England, and by Thorndike Press, USA.

Published in 2003 in the U.K. by arrangement with Constable & Robinson.

Published in 2003 in the U.S. by arrangement with Constable & Robinson Ltd.

U.K. Hardcover ISBN 0–7540–7259–2 (Chivers Large Print)
U.K. Softcover   ISBN 0–7540–7260–6 (Camden Large Print)
U.S. Softcover   ISBN 0–7862–5411–4 (Nightingale Series)

The text of this Large Print edition is unabridged.
Other aspects of the book may vary from the original edition.

Set in 16 pt. New Times Roman.

Printed in Great Britain on acid-free paper.

British Library Cataloguing in Publication Data available

Library of Congress Cataloging-in-Publication Data

Hunter, Alan.
    Over here / Alan Hunter.
        p.   cm.
    ISBN 0–7862–5411–4 (lg. print : sc : alk. paper)
    1. Gently, George (Fictitious character)—Fiction. 2. World War, 1939–1945—Veterans—Fiction. 3. Americans—England—Fiction. 4. Police—England—Fiction. 5. Fighter pilots—Fiction. 6. Large type books. I. Title.
PR6015.U565O94 2003
823'.914—dc21   2003047358

In Memory of my sister Evelyn

CHAPTER ONE

'George, there are some Americans in the village—they have come to look over the old airfield.'

It was April, and ranks of daffodils spread on each side of the lawn at Heatherings. A few white clouds were passing, but the sun fell warm on the front of the house; there was a mist of green on the beech-tree and the beech-hedging that enclosed the garden.

April—and a whole week before them!

They had left the flat in Kensington at seven that morning, Gently wearing his country tweeds, Gabrielle her new Spring outfit. At first the city traffic had been irksome but soon they had cleared the dreaded A25, and then they'd had a trouble-free run and had arrived in Welbourne by mid-morning. They had passed gorse in bloom, trees in tender new leaf, verges already white with cow parsley; and now, at Heatherings, sweeping over the lawn, the freshly-arrived martins were there to greet them.

Spring was in the air, in the sun, in Suffolk . . . there was even a yellow butterfly inspecting the daffodils.

'My dear, I have to go to the shop.'

Always, there was something Gabrielle had forgotten. But Gently preferred to laze in the

1

garden, to soak in the sun, the fragrance of the moment. Then he had lit his largest pipe and strolled to the gate in the beech hedge. From there he could gaze across the Walks to the distant church-tower of a neighbouring village, to the lines of greening birches, a farmhouse tucked away in trees.

'I asked about them in the shop. They are war-veterans, yes? They were stationed here in the war, and are come back to see the old places.'

Well, there wasn't much to see! The airfield had been in the next village, Toddington. It had been one of the hutted camps that had sprung up everywhere in Suffolk during the war, and afterwards to be abandoned and returned to agriculture. On some of the back roads round about one came upon the concrete remains of perimeter tracks and dispersals, and at one point a dishevelled Nissen hut, at another the ruin of what may have been a guard-room. Fifty years or more on . . . no, it wasn't much to come back to.

'Are they staying in Welbourne?'

'No. Mrs Cutting told me all about them. They stay in the Old Rectory guest-house at Toddington, and come here only to use our shop. There are six altogether, she says, and three have their wives with them. Two I saw, one with his wife, and this I tell you—she dyes her hair.'

'They'll be in their seventies at least . . .'

'Aha. But still good-looking men.'

'Are they here for long?'

'Till the end of the week. They have booked in the guest-house till then.'

'Pilots were they?'

'Yes. They were flying fighter-planes, Mrs Cutting says.'

Well, it added to the local colour, and Heatherings itself was not without a transatlantic connection. Formerly, it had been the home of a Colonel Jonson, of the U.S. Army Airforce.

'We may run into them.'

'I think, yes. I would like to meet that man's wife. They have two cars which they have rented, and each day they are seen in the village.'

Then the subject was dropped; and after lunch they took their favourite walk in the little valley, where the gorse was already incandescent, and where there was a chance of meeting with a nightingale. It was still too early for the little green butterflies, but Spring Beauty was in full flower, and a kestrel hovered above them as they made their way along the valley. Overhead the white clouds drifted peacefully, but never seemed to interrupt the gaze of the sun. They strolled, and loitered, and strolled afresh, till at last it was time to return to the house.

Mrs Jarvis had the table spread for them. She paused a moment when she brought the tea-tray.

'Daresay you've heard about them,' she said. 'Those Yanks they've got over at Toddington?'

'Yes, I am meeting them,' Gabrielle said.

Mrs Jarvis snorted. 'Hah. And you've heard the latest?'

'The latest . . . ?'

'Ah. About what they reckon to have found in one of those old huts. Mind you, I've only got it from Jack who does the garden, but he's usually up with the gossip.'

'And they found something?'

'So he says. Sticking up from out of the floor. Some bones, that's what it was, like there was a skeleton under there.'

'A skeleton!'

'So Jack says. Sticking up out of the floor. But it could be a sheep or anything, you know what people are like. I reckon it's just the Yanks having a game, or Jack pulling my leg. But there you are.'

Gently said: 'Do the police know of this?'

'He says they were out there this afternoon.'

'And that's all you've heard?'

'All he told me. But don't you worry, Mr Gently. If I didn't think it was all a game I wouldn't have bothered you with it.'

She poured the tea, and went back to her kitchen. Gabrielle was staring across at Gently.

'You think?'

Gently shrugged. 'Mrs Jarvis is probably

4

right!'

'But . . . if?'

'Drink your tea! In any case, it isn't my business.'

Gabrielle shook her head. 'You know best, my dear. But I do wish she hadn't told us about this.'

In the evening, in the normal way, they would probably have sauntered down to The Bell, but tonight Gently was careful not to make the suggestion. Over tea Gabrielle had remained thoughtful, clearly concerned by what they had heard, and in The Bell they could not have avoided joining in gossip about the rumour. In fact, he would have been the centre of it—his opinion sought, his information solicited! Instead, on the plea of it having been a long day, he settled down with a paper and the television.

'Tomorrow, we will call on Andy, yes?'

Reymerston was usually their first port of call.

'Perhaps I should ring him?'

'Don't bother. We are bound to find him at home.'

Because Andy, too, might have heard the rumour, and be eager to seek his opinion.

Restlessly, Gabrielle went to stare through the window, at the setting sun, the shadowy lawn; but in the end the television won, with a programme she had long been wishing to see. And finally Mrs Jarvis brought them their night-caps, and they retired with no further reference to Americans and rumours.

'It is so good to be home, my dear!'

And they slept soundly, with a window ajar.

*   *   *

'You'll find your mail on the table, Mr Gently. There's only the one letter.'

Monday brought another fine morning, with the sun brilliant on the nodding daffodils. They had risen early and, together, had gone down to stroll a few yards on the Walks. A light mist still clung to the slopes and hung about the dewy birches, while yesterday's pair of martins had now increased to six. But they hadn't lingered long.

'I have an appetite!'

Once, Gabrielle had scorned the English breakfast—it spoiled one's appetite for real meals, yes? A croissant and a cup of coffee should be all! By degrees, however, she had come to accept her bacon and egg, and even a bowl of porridge if it were properly made with the correct oatmeal.

The table was set ready, and the porridge was fetched as they took their places. Gently glanced at the letter casually, then picked it up with greater interest. A small, cheap envelope, it had the address written on it in crude capitals: he thumbed it open. It contained a single sheet, also inscribed with the same

6

capitals. The work of a child? He straightened it, and read:

'ASK THE YANKS ABOUT MILLY READ WENT MISSING 1944 AFTER A DANCE AT THE CAMP ONE WHO KNOWS'

A joke . . . ?

He turned the sheet over, but the reverse was blank. Cheap paper, scrawled letters, written with a coarse ball-pen. Frowning, he read it again.

'A letter from one of your admirers, George?'

He shook his head.

'May your wife see?'

What could he do? Reluctantly, he passed the note to her. Gabrielle stared at it, at first with amusement, then with a face grown suddenly grave.

'But—my dear!'

'It could be only a joke. We get people sending us these things all the time.'

'But there is a name here—a date.'

'It may be only someone wanting to stir up trouble.'

'No—I cannot believe!'

'Yes. It happens.'

'But they find these bones!'

'We don't know the full story. They could be those of an animal, as Mrs Jarvis says, and this note someone's misguided idea of humour.'

She stared at the note, at him, then shook

her head. 'I think you say that to please me, my friend. You, you do not think this is a joke. Something I am sure you will be doing about it.'

Gently sighed. Yes—he would! A jest or no, it required attention. But not by him. If the note had any consequence, then it was the business of the local C.I.D. Today Andy Reymerston must go on hold while they made a trip into Wolmering.

'So, then?'

'We'll go into town, and I'll give this note to our friend Eyke. And in the meantime we will forget about it and try to remember that we are on holiday.'

'Seriously, you do not think . . . ?'

'I think our porridge is getting cold!'

He took the note from her, stuffed it back in its envelope, and the envelope in his wallet.

Gabrielle sighed too, but picked up her spoon and made a start on her porridge.

But the note had thrown a shadow on that sunny morning, and the meal progressed in silence. A name had been given, a date, the hint of a tragedy of long ago. An imagined tragedy? That was possible! A connection where perhaps there was no connection, a memory of some event brought suddenly to mind by the rumoured discovery . . . On the other hand . . . Gently pushed his plate aside and helped himself to more coffee.

'Don't expect us to lunch, Mrs Jarvis. We

8

shall probably have it out.'

'It was only chops, Mr Gently. And they'll keep till tonight.'

He filled a pipe and went outside to wipe the Rover's dewy windscreen. Overhead the martins were hovering by their nests, under the eaves. Gabrielle joined him, and paused to look at the martins before reluctantly, silently, getting into the car.

*   *   *

'Drop me here, my dear. You don't need me to come in with you. I shall take a look at the shops, and then have my coffee at The Pelican.'

April was astir in Wolmering too, in the busy High Street, the crowded pavements. The clothes the women wore were more colourful, men were strolling without their jackets. Easter was at hand. Here and there, shop-fronts were decorated with coloured tinsels. A banner, slung between two of the buildings, advertised a concert on the Easter Monday.

Patiently Gently threaded his way along the High Street, here and there pausing to give way to other traffic. In '44, wouldn't the Americans have frequented this small, fashionable sea-side town? At most it was eight miles from the airfield, a natural target for liberty-wagons, with its hotels, pubs, cinema, and dances organised in the town hall.

And girls of course: their men were away in Italy, North Africa, or guarding the convoys. Overpaid, over-sexed and over here! Yes, there must be tales to tell in Wolmering . . .

He shrugged to himself and made his turn into the street leading to the police station.

'Is Inspector Eyke available?'

'If you would just state your business, sir . . .'

The man at the desk was a stranger, who regarded Gently impatiently.

'I require a word with the Inspector.'

'I'm afraid he's too busy this morning, sir.'

'I think he may find time to see me.'

And Gently laid his warrant on the counter.

He interrupted Eyke and his side-kick, Metfield, brooding over what appeared to be a forensic report. The local man rose quickly to hold out his hand.

'Sorry about that, sir! Benson is new here, and we do have a flap on. Something turned up yesterday that's got everyone in a lather.'

'It wouldn't be something to do with Toddington?'

'Then you've heard—?'

'I've heard a rumour.'

'If only that's all it was, sir!' Eyke shook his head bitterly. 'No, sir. We've got a case on. And I'm hanged if I know how we're going to tackle it.'

'Then those bones weren't the bones of a sheep.'

'They bloody weren't—if you'll excuse my

grammar!'

'So?'

Eyke indicated the report. 'The bones of a female, aged around twenty, who probably died fifty years ago. The state of some of the clothing found with her told them that. And then there's the pay-off. A bust hyoid bone.'

'She was . . . strangled.'

Eyke nodded miserably. 'And somehow we've got to take it from there. A ruddy homicide that must have happened before Metty here was born.'

'May I see that report?'

Eyke handed it to him, then lit and puffed tensely at a cheroot. The girl had been five foot-four, of slim build, and recovered hair showed that she had been a blonde. As far as forensic could reconstruct the clothing, she had been wearing a coat over a long-hemmed dress, both stained with oil from engine-covers under which the body had been found. No handbag or any identification was discovered. The skeleton was slightly compressed by the weight of concrete slabs placed over it, but the only certain injury was the fracture of the hyoid bone. Gently handed back the report.

'When was the discovery reported to you?'

'Yesterday, at around eleven. We had a call from that guest-house out there where they've got these Yanks staying. An old boy called Major Forrest. It was two of his pals who spotted the bones. They'd been out together

11

looking round the old place, and went into this Nissen hut, which they remembered from way back. The concrete floor is bust at one corner and there was a slab on the tilt, and they could see the bones of a foot sticking out. According to them they didn't interfere with anything, just went and told the others what they'd found.'

'When did you get out there?'

'Straight away, me and Metty. It was how they said, the foot sticking out, and you could see a bit of the leg bone too. I called in forensic directly, and took statements from the two buffers who found her. Forensic got the concrete off her, and some old engine-covers, and there she lay.'

'Aircraft engine-covers?'

'So they say.' Eyke gave Gently a keen look. 'You reckon?'

Gently nodded. 'If they were oil-soaked they would help to conceal any odour.'

'Yeah.' Eyke chewed his cheroot.

'Is the Nissen hut used for anything these days?'

'No. I talked to the farmer. It's too far off from the farmyard, and it's stood derelict as long as he remembers. The door is off its hinges and two of the windows are knocked out. The Yanks say it wasn't far from their mess-hall in the old days, but now it just stands alone in the corner of a wood.'

'Empty.'

'Well . . . it is now!' Eyke stubbed the cheroot and drew a deep breath. 'And where the hell I'm supposed to start looking I just do not know. Chummie did a good job. He disposed of the body. And all that was fifty years ago. We don't know who, and we don't know when. That sodding report says it all.'

'But . . . a name might help?'

Eyke stared.

'And perhaps a date?'

Eyke's stare widened.

Slowly, Gently took out his wallet and handed the letter to Eyke.

'This came in the post this morning. Apparently someone round here was acquainted with the victim.'

*　　　*　　　*

Eyke fumbled the letter open, glared at it, then sank back on his chair.

'Bloody . . . hell.'

Shamelessly, over Eyke's shoulder, Metfield was also staring at the letter.

'I'm afraid it's been handled,' Gently said. 'Both by myself and my wife. But there's still a chance that you may be able to get a dab from it. The postmark is indecipherable, but the letter must have caught yesterday's collection. That means it was written by somebody local who had heard the rumour of what had been found, and somebody who also knew that the

13

Americans were staying here.'

'So that makes it the body of a local girl, sir,' Metfield said.

'That's fairly certain.'

'And the geezer who wrote that must have known her.'

Gently nodded.

'Some oldie still living here ...'

'Yes. I think that's a safe assumption.'

'He might even be family!'

Gently shrugged. 'The text doesn't suggest it, but it might be worth checking on any Reads in the vicinity. Also, of course, on the record of missing persons for that year.'

Eyke snatched up the envelope and scowled at it. 'I don't know, sir,' he said. 'It could just be a lark by someone who's got it in for the Yanks.'

'That's always possible.'

'Some nutter who wants us to give them a hard time. Because if he really does know something, why doesn't he just come forward and say so?'

'He may have reasons.'

'I can't think what, sir. Unless it's him we should be looking for.'

'And it doesn't have to be a "him".'

Eyke stared at Gently, then at the letter.

Gently said: 'Both the content and the writing rather suggest an elderly lady, it might even be one who, in the year quoted, used to frequent the dances she speaks of. In that case

14

she may have critical testimony, and you will need to lay your hands on her.'

'But it could as well be an old bloke, sir.'

'Either way, you need to talk to them. But first of all, check the record for a missing person called Millicent Read.'

Eyke sighed feelingly. 'Don't you worry, sir. We're going to check this one out. I'll be on to Eastwich right away, and Metty can search the rolls for any Reads.' He hesitated. 'Will you be in touch, sir?'

'I'll look in later, if I may.'

'You know the answer to that one, sir! And thanks for getting this to me so soon.'

Outside Gently paused to light a pipe before strolling back to the busy High Street. It was true: from his first sight of it, he had the intuition that the letter emanated from a woman. A jealous woman, a woman with a grudge, remembered after all these years . . . 'one who knows!' But, if she knew, what had stopped her giving testimony at the time?

Local she had to be, to know of himself and his address in Welbourne, and that he was presently in residence there and not at the flat in Kensington. A local resident in Welbourne or Toddington, which was only a short distance down the road: a resident of long-standing, of a period stretching back to war days, and perhaps beyond. A woman in her seventies . . . his mind's eye wandered over familiar faces in the village, but none seemed quite to fit, to

15

match the tone, the act, of the letter.

Ah well . . . leave it to Eyke!

He headed for the shops that would attract Gabrielle—fashion, books, the one that specialised in amber; to catch her at last in the coffee-lounge of The Pelican.

'I thought you had forgotten me, my dear!'

Very briefly, he gave an outline of what he had learned at the police station, the fact that the remains were those of a young girl and that foul play had to be accepted. She heard him large-eyed.

'And—they suspect those Americans?'

'As yet, they have no suspect.'

'But the letter is saying . . . ?'

He shook his head. 'They have yet to discover and interrogate the writer.'

Gabrielle stared at her cup. 'I do not know! This is happening, it says, after one of their dances. They would have been young men under great stresses, and if this foolish girl had played one of them false?'

'That . . . is one possibility.'

'But yes. Ask the Yanks, is what it is saying.'

'The jealousy may have been on the part of the writer.'

'The writer? I cannot think so!'

He ordered coffee too, and for a while they sat silent, staring out of the window at the busy pavement. Then she turned to him again.

'And now, my dear, you wish to stay in town? You will be holding the hand of poor

Eyke?'

Gently grimaced. 'Not quite like that! But he is expecting me to call back.'

'Then, my dear, you shall. I met with Andy in the High. I am telling him why you come here, and he says, should I need it, he will give me a lift home.'

So it was arranged: in due course Reymerston collected her from The Pelican. For a while, Gently sat on, through a couple of pipes and another coffee, then, after several glances at his watch, rose and set off back to the police-station.

'The Chief Inspector is waiting, sir . . .'

In the office he found Eyke on the phone. After a number of terse exchanges, he hung up with a slam.

'This you are not going to believe, sir! That tart we are after came from Bakewell.'

'From Bakewell . . . ?'

'In Derbyshire. I've just been on to the locals up there.'

'Then she wasn't from round here?'

Eyke shook his head. 'Metty has checked all the Reads for miles. The nearest family is in Harford, and they know nothing of any missing relatives.'

Gently pulled up a chair, and sat. 'But you'll have got some more detail from Records?'

'That's just the point, sir. We've got next to nothing. They tell me Records was hit by a flying bomb, and most of the early stuff was destroyed. They sent me a fax of what they'd got, a final report of the officer involved, but it's just a write-off. They seem to have thought she'd done a bunk, either on her own or with some bloke. It gives us a date, January 30th '44, and her home address. But that's the lot. I did enquire whether the officer was still around, but they told me he passed on quite a few years back.'

'They have no information about what she was doing here.'

'No sir. I'm hoping Bakewell can give us a line on that.'

'Did the report include her age?'

'She was twenty, sir.'

'Twenty ... in 1944.'

Eyke hesitated. 'You're thinking, sir ... ?'

Gently nodded. 'She had probably been called up. And the odds would be that she was in the WAAF, stationed at one of the RAF camps about here. In that case, the Air Ministry might have records.'

Eyke looked doubtful. 'May be worth a try, sir. But the army had bases round here too, and we had the Navy using the harbour.'

Gently shrugged. 'And there's the other angle! Someone resident in Welbourne or Toddington was acquainted with Millicent Read. Quite well-acquainted is my impression, as though at one time they may have been mates together, perhaps sharing the same quarters and engaged in the same duties.' He

18

paused. 'Were there dabs on that letter?'

'Yes sir. But I can't see them getting us far.'

'The paper is the sort sold in the village shop. It might just be worth enquiring who has bought some lately.'

'I'll bear it in mind, sir.' But Eyke didn't sound hopeful.

'If I may, I would like to look at that fax.'

Eyke passed it over. The report was minimal and dated some while after the incident, written by hand: an impatient resumé undertaken to replace records destroyed by the bombing. No witnesses were named, just the simple fact of the girl being last seen when she left the dancing, an affair proceeding in the officers' mess, with the addition that the bicycle she was known to have arrived on was missing from the place where it had been left. As Eyke had said, the impression given was that her departure and subsequent disappearance had been voluntary. No mention was included of her occupation, merely name, age and home address. Gently passed the fax back.

'Bakewell had no memory of such an incident?'

'Not the ones I spoke to, sir. But they did say they knew of some local Read families, and promised they would look into it for us.'

'It would have been them who passed on the news, and checked that the girl had not returned home. And it may just have made the local papers, both at Bakewell and back here.'

Eyke shook his head. 'There was a war on, sir! But I'll ask Eastwich to make a check.'

'And that leaves us with the advice in the letter.'

'You mean, sir . . . ?'

Gently nodded. 'Ask the Yanks.'

Eyke looked down his nose. 'I suppose we have to, sir. Though I was hoping we could get by without it . . .'

Gently said: 'They were around at that time. They are familiar with the layout as it was. They may well have been at that dance. Some may even recall Millicent Read.'

'Yes sir. But it looks—you know!'

'It would look as though we had them under suspicion?'

'Well . . . yes, sir. A bit like that. And them a lot of oldies, with their wives along with them.'

Slowly, Gently shrugged. 'It's a risk we'll have to take! They have information, and we can't overlook it. So perhaps you'll just ring that guest-house and arrange for them to receive a visit.'

'You mean—us, sir?'

'If you'd like to have me along.'

Still Eyke hesitated, staring at the phone. Finally, he picked it up and dialled, with an expression that was not his happiest.

20

CHAPTER TWO

The call was taken by the same Major Forrest who had reported the discovery. Apparently the senior member of the party, he agreed to have as many of them as he could contact assembled in the guest-house lounge at noon. He had asked no questions, Eyke said, just listened to the request and made the arrangement. It sounded a little as though he were expecting it, perhaps was wondering why it hadn't happened before.

'You have met him, of course.'

'Yes sir. A lean old cove of around eighty. But he can still handle himself, and he's got his head screwed on.'

'Of course, they'll have discussed it among themselves.'

'Bound to have done, sir.'

'They may have some answers waiting for us ... and then again, they may not.'

'You mean—they'll be covering for each other, sir?'

'At least, they'll be playing it close to their chests. A group of old comrades in a foreign country. We can't expect them to tell tales on each other.'

'No sir ... I suppose not.'

Gently shrugged. 'And meanwhile, we just have time for a pint!'

The Horseshoes was nearest, and accompanied by Metfield they took their drinks in a near-empty bar. Then, with Metfield driving them in a squad-car, they set out to cover the few miles to Toddington.

Compared with Welbourne, Toddington was a hamlet, grouped largely around its church and pub. It possessed a small post-office, but no shop, and one passed through it quickly to the open country beyond. Here, half a mile out, a narrow road bore right, to be joined by one yet narrower; and a hundred yards down the latter brought them to the gates and drive of the Old Rectory. A large, Edwardian brick building, with numerous sash-windows and a feature porch, it stood among lawns and guardian beech trees, an occupied island in the surrounding fields. In front of the house two cars were parked. On the steps of the porch, a tall figure was waiting.

'That's him—Major Forrest.'

He came down the steps to meet them, a lanky, hawkish-featured man with thinning grey hair and frank grey eyes. Eighty? He must have been near it, but it scarcely showed in his easy motions. He was dressed in a stylish worsted suit, the effect a little spoiled by white-panelled trainers.

'Hiya—Inspector Eyke, isn't it?' He held out a steady hand. 'And this gentleman you have with you?'

Awkwardly, Eyke performed the

22

introduction.

'Gently—that's an unusual name.' But clearly it meant nothing to him. He shook hands, and again with Metfield, whose name he also remembered from the previous occasion.

'Well now, I guess we could have met up on a cheerfuller business than this is, but I've got the fellas lined up for you, all except Bill Mitchell, who's off some place with his wife. You got some specific questions to put to us?'

'Perhaps—one or two!' Eyke stammered.

'And you, Gently, you're in on this?'

Gently merely bowed his head.

'Yeah—well.' Major Forrest frowned. 'On a set-up like this we have to expect it. The shame is it had to happen to us, on what would have been the last trip over for most of us. But that's life I guess. And things weren't so rosy the first time we came to these parts. So let's get on, fellas, and hear what you've dug up to ask us.'

He led the way in. A handsome tiled hall brought them to the large lounge, a room with a run of tall windows looking out on a lawn and rose-beds. There four elderly men were seated, in the company of two elderly ladies. Three of the four men had glasses in their hands, while the ladies had a coffee-tray between them. Major Forrest closed the door behind them. He gestured to the policemen.

'Well, here we are, folks! Two of these

23

gentlemen you've met already. This other one is a Mr Gently, and my guess is he's a top man they've called in. That right, Gently?'

Gently bowed. 'Unofficially,' he said.

'But you're in on it, ain't that so?'

'I'm here to give any assistance I can.'

'Yeah, yeah.' Major Forrest nodded. 'So now we know where we stand, folks. We've got some HQ brass on the job.' He hesitated. 'What do you say we start off with a little drink?'

'Not for me,' Gently said.

'Then you other guys?'

Eyke and Metfield shook their heads.

'So maybe later,' Major Forrest said. 'But you can pour one for me, Chuck. Me, I've always found interrogation to be dry work.'

A square-featured man with bushy grey hair reached out to a tray to fill a glass. Nursing it, Major Forrest took a seat in a chair by the two ladies, one a hefty woman with wavy dyed hair, the other slimmer. With darker dye.

'So—who kicks off?'

Eyke looked at Gently, and Metfield through the window. Gently said: 'To waste no time, we have identified the remains that two of you discovered. She was a twenty-year-old girl from another part of the country. But, on January 30th, 1944, she was attending a dance at Toddington Camp, a dance held in the Officers' Mess. And on that night she disappeared.'

A sudden silence in the room!

'You—you're sure of your facts?' Major Forrest demanded.

'Quite sure.'

'And you've got your dates right?'

'The dates are on record.'

'So what was the name of this young bird?'

'Her name—' Gently paused '—was Millicent Read, better known to her friends as Milly.'

No one spoke. There was a clinking sound as the dark lady nervously put down her cup.

* * *

Gently looked round at the four men, but none of them seemed willing to meet his eye. All were elderly, in their seventies, though one of them was sporting auburn hair. Another was unashamedly balding, a third wearing his grey locks in a style. The bushy-haired one was clad in an anorak, the others more conventionally. It was Major Forrest who broke the silence. He took a quick nip.

'See here, Gently. All this was going on fifty years back, you got to make some allowances, hey? Things we remember, things we don't. Sure, there were shenanigans in the mess. But our business here was flying P-51's alongside the Libbys and Forts. That's what sticks in the memory, fella, those trips out to Bremen, Berlin and the rest. And like counting the ones

25

who didn't come back. That's one of them, sitting over there.' He waved his glass towards the balding man. 'You tell him, Kit,' he said. 'How you were shot down over Gelsenkirchen, and spent the next eighteen months in a stalag.'

The balding man's shoulder twitched. 'I'd sooner forget all that, Rob,' he said. 'I was one of the lucky ones who came back, unlike Stew and a few more.'

'It was flack that got you, wasn't it?'

The balding man shook his head.

'Came down in a ditch?'

He shrugged.

'You get my point,' Major Forrest said. 'Those are the things that stick, Gently, not the dolls who came to our hops. Sure, we whooped it up when we could, but the next day we were tangling with Heinkels and Messerschmidts. It was war, and you lived one day at a time. All the rest was like a dream.'

Slowly Gently nodded. 'Yet . . . dreams sometimes stay in the memory. And some of those dolls you mentioned did wind up as GI brides.'

'Not here. Not with any of my men.'

Gently let his gaze stray round the room. They found the dark lady. She was staring hard at the bushy-haired man, whose eyes were fixed on his glass. Then she felt Gently's eyes on her and transferred her stare to the window.

Gently said: 'Your unit was stationed here for how long?'

'Maybe a year,' Major Forrest said.

'And these dances—perhaps once a week?'

'I guess. Sometimes more often.'

'And one would have been on the date I mentioned?'

'Yeah . . . we were here through '44.'

'Were they functions that you yourself attended?'

He glanced at the wavy-haired woman. 'Guess I did.'

'And others here present?'

Major Forrest made a face.

'So,' Gently said. 'Once a week or more these dances were held in the mess, attended by yourselves and girls invited from the neighbourhood. They would be mostly the same girls, since this is a lightly-populated area, and in the natural course of events you must have become well-acquainted with them. Then, one of these girls disappears, and enquiries about her are made by the police. With due acknowledgement to your arduous duties, can none of you here bring that girl to mind?'

There were uneasy shuffling noises. The dark lady's stare had returned to the bushy-haired man.

Gently said: 'A blonde-haired girl of medium height. Millicent Read. Milly.'

'Oh, what the heck!'—It was the balding

27

man from whom the utterance came, and having made it, he crouched a little forward, his gaze fixed on the carpet.

'You do remember her, sir?'

'My name is Pederson, if you want to know! And yes, I do remember her. It was the day after that dance I was shot down.'

'You perhaps remember that night very well.'

'I danced with her twice. That's all.'

'She was a girl you knew.'

'Yeah, yeah. We met her at a pub when we first came here.'

'We?'

'Me and some other fellas! She was there with a pal, a work-mate of hers. We were looking for talent for the mess-dance, and invited the two of them along. Milly came, her pal didn't. I guess she had her reasons.'

'Then Miss Read was working in these parts?'

'Sure, I thought you'd know that. She was one of those—what did they call them? Used to wear plus-fours and a green sweater.'

'You mean—a Land Girl?'

'Yeah, that's it. She worked on a farm round here some place. And her pal worked there too, though what her name was I don't remember.'

'Or the farm?'

'Don't think I ever knew it, but it couldn't have been far. She used to ride here on her bike.'

Gently paused and looked at the others. Once more, they preferred to elude his gaze. Finally, the dark lady made a jerking movement, sat up straighter in her chair.

'Chuck, for heaven's sake!'

'Rita . . .'

'Well, if you don't tell him, I will!' Her brown eyes fixed on Gently's. She said: 'Yessir. My husband there knew that little number.'

'Your husband . . . ?'

'Chuck Osborne—First Looey and all that crap. I saw the letters he wrote home to his ma, and sure, he mentioned the blonde babe.'

'Rita, that's not fair—!'

'Don't kid me, Chuck. I'll bet you laid her and a dozen others. And you'd got me waiting at home, on pins in case a telegram arrived. Was that being fair?'

'She wasn't a tart either!'

'Her, and the rest of the babes at those dances.'

'No, you've got it wrong!'

'There was a war on, ain't that the excuse?'

'Here, here!' Major Forrest broke in. 'No need to carry on that way, Rita. I was there. I ran those dances. Guess they weren't the kinda orgies you seem to think.'

'Huh. And huh again.'

'They were decent girls, they were doing their bit. So you pipe down, my lady, and stop giving this man the wrong impression.'

Rita Osborne gave a snatch of her head, but bit her lip and said no more. Her husband kneaded his glass and stared at the contents, his features flushed.

Gently said: 'Then you, too, were acquainted with her?'

He made a motion with the glass. 'Guess I was. But she wasn't the slag Rita is saying, not Milly. She kept her drawers on.'

'A respectable girl.'

'I guess. She liked her fun, but it stopped there. Like she was an educated kinda girl, one you could talk to. A pal.'

'A good-looker?'

'I'll say that. A pretty, intelligent sorta face. And that blonde hair tied up with a ribbon. Got a figure too. And she could dance.'

'Had she a boyfriend?'

'Maybe.'

'Someone you knew?'

He frowned at the glass. 'Just maybe! I never did ask her. But a girl like that surely had admirers.'

Had his eye drifted a moment towards Pederson? He took a quick pull from the glass. Still a handsome fellow, though in his seventies, tall, square-featured, hazel-eyed. And Pederson . . .? He had put on weight, showed a trace of jowl in his fleshy face.

'I guess we all fancied Milly—the guys queued up to ask her to dance!'

The speaker was the auburn-haired man, a

30

perky-faced fellow who grinned as he spoke. Perhaps a year or two younger than the others, he was shorter, and slighter in build.

'You speak for yourself, Jacko!'

'Well wasn't that so, if you put it on the line? I fancied her rotten when she turned up. The snag was, she would never look at me.'

'You fancied every dame rotten.'

'Yeah, but Milly was the peach. We could have gone places, her and me, if I could have gotten her seeing it my way.'

'So she had the sense to turn you down.'

'Yeah. And then look at the dames I did marry.'

'Come off it, Spicer,' Major Forrest said sharply. 'We can count up your divorces another day.'

Spicer grimaced and was silent. Osborne threw back the dregs from his glass. Gently said:

'I would like to come now to that dance in January when Miss Read was last seen alive. How many of you here would have been present at the dance?'

There was a pause. They looked at each other. Rita Osborne poured herself another drop of coffee.

*　　　*　　　*

'We were all there, I guess.'

It was the fourth man who had spoken, the

31

one with the styled grey hair. He had lined, drawn features, and was dressed in a suit, with a bow-tie.

'My name is Clifton. And the Major was mistaken when he said we had no GI brides on this station. I met my late wife, Mary, at one of these dances, and we were married in the church here in the Spring of '44.'

'Sorry, Larry!' Major Forrest said. 'Guess I thought you wouldn't want me to bring that up.'

Clifton's head sank. 'It's O.K., Rob. I've learned to live with it these few years.'

Gently said: 'And you were present at the dance in question?'

He nodded. 'I remember it well, because Mary was late. She was held up by some business at her office and didn't arrive till the dance was half over.'

'You remember seeing Miss Read there?'

'Yes.'

'You perhaps danced with her?'

He shook his head. 'I didn't dance. I was there to meet Mary. I spent my time at the bar, and keeping an eye on the door. When she got there we danced a couple, and sat another one out. Then we sat a while in her little car. I guess it was midnight when we broke up.'

'Would you have seen the others leaving?'

'Some.'

'Including Miss Read?'

'I . . . guess not.'

'Was she still in the mess when you and your friend left?'

He simply shook his head. 'I'd never have noticed. It was just . . . Mary and me. We snuck out and went to the car. When I left Mary the joint had closed down, and I went straight back to quarters.'

Gently paused. He said: 'I understand the Nissen hut where the remains were found was no great distance from the mess. Is it possible you may have had it in view from where you were seated in the car?'

'No. That hut was back of the mess. The parking was on the other side.'

'But you would be able to see people leaving the mess?'

'Guess I would. If I'd been watching.'

'You remember nothing of that.'

'No. Like I said . . . it was just her and me.'

Major Forrest said: 'If I remember right that hut was full of junk the RAF had left there. We never did sort it out. The guys used it to stash their bikes.'

'Bikes were left there?'

He nodded.

Gently said: 'We know that Miss Read arrived at the camp on her bike, and that afterwards the bike was missing. Is it likely she would have left it in the Nissen hut?'

'More than likely, I guess.'

'So she would have gone there later to collect it?'

Major Forrest said nothing. Nobody wanted to catch Gently's eye.

Gently said: 'Getting back to the dance! Were any of you here her partners that night?'

'Me, I tried to grab her,' Spicer smirked. 'But that babe just handed me off real smart.'

'And you others?'

'Oh heck!' Pederson growled. 'Like I told you, I had two goes with her—the waltz was one. And maybe the rumba. But I danced with a few other chicks too.'

'Was it early or late in the evening?'

'Hell, it was fifty-three years ago.'

'Did she talk to you?'

'Guess she did.'

'Do you remember what about?'

'Maybe—stockings.'

'Stockings . . . ?'

'The dames were crazy about them,' Major Forrest put in. 'Nylon stockings. They couldn't buy them here, but we got them through our PX.'

Gently shook his head. 'And you promised her a pair?'

'Maybe. I don't remember.'

'And that was the only subject of your conversation?'

Pederson made a pretence of spitting.

Gently said: 'Your two dances with Miss Read. Was it the waltz or the rumba which was the latest?'

'You go to hell!'

34

'Is it possible that one was the last dance of the evening?'

Pederson stuck out his chin and was silent.

'Does anyone remember?' Gently said. 'Who it was had the last dance with Miss Read?'

'Should have been me,' Spicer grinned. 'But somehow I guess it wasn't.'

'Anyone?'

He looked round. Pederson couldn't help it: he was glancing towards Osborne.

* * *

For a moment Osborne ignored him. He still had the empty glass in his hand. Then he sighed, reached across to set the glass back on its tray.

'It was me,' he said. 'I had the last dance with her. Only it wasn't the last dance—she had to leave early. Some deal about milking cows the next morning.'

'She told you that?'

'I'm saying. We had the last dance but one. I tried to get her to stay on, but no. Like the cows came first with Milly.'

Gently paused. 'Would you have seen her out?'

Osborne gave the vestige of a nod. 'I fetched her coat and helped her on with it. Then I went out front with her.'

'Just out front?'

'Just out front. We may have had a word out there, but that's all. Conscientious she was. She had to get back for those goddamn cows.'

'Then—she went for her bike.'

His lips were tight. 'Yeah.'

'You saw her depart towards the hut.'

'I saw her.' His hands were gripped into two fists.

'So . . . you were the last person to see her alive.'

'For Chrissake fella—leave it out!' The fists slammed together. 'Can't you imagine what I've been thinking all this time? If I had gone with her, this wouldn't have happened, and she'd maybe still be alive today. But no, she would have me go back in, told me I was missing the last dance.'

'She sent you back in.'

'Right.'

'You last saw her on her way to the hut.'

'I'm telling you.'

'And—no other person in the vicinity at the time?'

'If so, I didn't see them.'

Gently nodded. 'So you went back in, presumably in time for the last dance. Is it possible that you would have noticed if anyone was absent from the mess just then?'

'Anyone . . . ?'

'Among those lining up for that last dance?'

Osborne stared at him, eyes wide. Then his gaze sank to his knees.

'Well?'

'I don't remember!'

'No face missing just then?'

'No. If there were . . .'

'Yes?'

'Like I said—I don't remember!'

Gently eyed him steadily. 'Are you sure of that, Mr Osborne?'

'For crying out loud!'

'Quite sure?'

He jerked his face away from Gently's.

'Hell's bells, stop hounding the poor guy!' —It was Pederson who interrupted. 'Yeah, sure there was someone missing, but he ain't going to tell you. That guy was me.'

'You, Mr Pederson?'

'You heard me.' His scowling eyes fixed on Gently's. 'And I guess it's time we got this straight, fella. He was sweet on Milly. And so was I.'

'You were both admirers of Miss Read?'

'I'm saying. She was the swellest babe around. She got enough nylon stockings from us to set up a harem, if she'd wanted. She was kinda special, Milly was, and we were both on our knees. So now you know, fella. And you can write that down in your book.'

'You were—rivals, for her affection.'

'Yeah. And me, I was getting the air.'

'She preferred Mr Osborne?'

'That's how it went.'

There was a gasp from Rita Osborne!

Gently said: 'You saw them leaving, and at that point you absented yourself from the mess?'

Pederson spat. 'I wanted space, fella, time out. To be where I wouldn't see them smooching.'

'So—where did you go?'

'I hit the toilets.'

'Those would be the toilets in the mess?'

'Nope. Outside at the rear. As far from the love-birds as I could get.'

Gently paused. 'And you stayed there how long?'

He spat. 'Till I'd smoked a cheroot, I guess. Till the music stopped. Till I reckoned that Milly would be on her way.'

'Perhaps twenty minutes?'

'Maybe.'

'Alone?'

'If I said different you couldn't disprove it.'

Gently stared at him, nodded. 'And after that you returned to the mess?'

'Yeah,' Pederson growled. 'I felt I needed a drink. Only I found Chuck propping up the bar, and I guess I didn't feel palsy just then. I swallowed a quick one and blew. And now you've heard the whole story.'

'When you were outside, you saw no one?'

He shook his head, and looked away.

Major Forrest cleared his throat. 'See here, Gently,' he said. 'Your guys went into this at the time, and they got nowhere with the

38

business. We were all put through it except Kit, who wasn't here to be questioned, and the notion they came up with was that the girl had levanted with a fella. That was how it looked. Chuck had seen her off, and her bike was gone from the hut. Like she'd got another iron in the fire, was just kidding our two boys along.'

Gently shrugged. 'It could have looked that way.'

'Sure. It was war time and these things happened. So now we know different, but I guess it's too late to figure what really went on back there. Wouldn't you say?'

'You may be right.'

Major Forrest nodded decidedly. 'Of course, we're here to answer your questions and give you any help we can, but miracles you cannot expect. Fifty-three years is a very long time. I'll just say, as one who was present at the dance that night, that I can back up what the fellas have told you, and they've given you the facts as I know them. O.K. with you?'

'O.K.'. Gently found him a smile. 'Just one other small thing, and then I'll leave you people to your lunch.'

'Whatever you want.'

'To the best of your memories, I would like a sketch-map of the area of the mess, showing the position of the Nissen-hut, the parking, and anything else that comes to mind.'

They looked at each other. 'Fine,' Major Forrest said. 'I guess we should be able to manage that. Fetch me that pad from the hall, Jacko. And I'll borrow your pen, my dear.'

The pad was fetched, and the wavy-haired lady produced a ball-pen from her bag. The others gathered round to watch the Major rapidly sketch in a series of rectangles and lines. When it was done, he handed it round, but nobody suggested any revisions. After carefully labelling the salient features, he tore off the sheet and handed it to Gently.

'And the position of the toilets . . . ?'

'Give it here!' Pederson almost snarled.

The toilets were duly added and the sheet handed back to Gently.

'O.K. now?'

Gently nodded. 'And my thanks to you all for your assistance.'

'Any time,' Major Forrest said. 'Any time. We shall be around here till the end of the week. Can I offer you a drink now?'

Gently shook his head, and the session was ended. Major Forrest accompanied them out to the steps and again took Gently's hand. He held on to it a moment, frowning.

'You getting ideas in there, Gently?' he said.

'Just gathering facts.'

'Those boys flew with me. I'd swear to the characters of every last one of them.'

Gently bowed his head.

'They were heroes,' Major Forrest said. 'Even Spicer and his trail of women.'

And he remained on the steps gazing after

40

them as they drove away down the gravelled drive.

CHAPTER THREE

'I owe you one, sir!'

At the first junction Gently had signalled Metfield to turn left, and they began to unravel a narrow, winding road between hawthorn hedges and fields green with young crops. Here and there copses intervened, and at one point a belt of woodland. Primroses flourished on hedge-banks and oaks were sherbet-coloured with young growth.

'I don't mind admitting I was dreading that job, but you handled it a treat. Were you getting it down, Metty?'

In a corner of the room Metfield had been scribbling away at a pad, catching dirty looks from Major Forrest, but unnoticed by most of the others.

'The best part, sir. I think I've got everything that counts.'

'We can get their statements later. We'll have them into the office for that. If you ask me we got somewhere just now, and that old bird of a Major knows it. What do you think, sir?'

'I think he's worried.'

'Worried stiff I'd say, sir!'

41

'As yet we're only beginning to get the picture.'

Eyke shook his head. 'It's looking pretty clear to me, sir.'

And perhaps it was. What they had unearthed bore all the appearance of a classic case, of jealousy reaching a point where it had led to violent crime. One had been chosen, one denied. In a setting where none knew what the morrow might bring. Where, in fact, one of the protagonists had been shot from the skies on the day after the crime . . .

Yet Gently found himself frowning.

Could it be because all this had happened five decades ago?

The Major had not been slow to point out that there had been a full inquiry at the time, when the evidence, the testimony was fresh, and elements to hand that were absent now. The same picture was available then but apparently had led to no definite conclusion. On the facts the girl had probably taken herself off, it may have been on some other, undisclosed, romantic adventure.

And, if nothing had been proved then, what chance was there now, under the weight of such a passage of years . . . ?

'Did you put a man on tracing the source of that anonymous note?'

'Yes sir. I put Campsey on the job. But I reckon it was only someone stirring up the gossip, perhaps some old dear who was around

42

at the time.'

'They may still have testimony that could be useful.'

'I'm sure Campsey will do his best, sir.'

But failing that? Gently shrugged to himself. Suspicion was one thing, proof another. He signalled another left turn, into another anonymous country way.

'We're . . . going to look at the scene, sir?'

'We're going to look at the scene.'

No one needed to tell Gently where it was. On his explorations of the country around Welbourne he had several times noticed the lonely Nissen hut and other remnants of the airfield. In fact they had already passed some, areas of concrete overgrown with bushes, at one point extending into a field and to a dump of manure, surrounded by tyre-marks. Dispersal points . . . a perimeter-track? There had gone the P-51 fighters, the Pedersons, the Osbornes, on their consort-duties with the bombers, some never again to touch down on the beckoning concrete of the Suffolk fields. What were the thoughts of those veterans who returned here to discover, if they could, one familiar aspect?

'Here we are, sir . . .'

Yes. The hut still nestled under a gloom of trees, back from the road, behind a fret of concrete that bore signs of recent traffic. And the rest—the messes, the offices, the canteen, the quarters? As far as could be seen not a trace remained: just bushes, trees, the surrounding fields. The hut alone was left to represent Toddington Camp, its broken windows, lapsing door and flaking green paintwork.

Metfield drove in and parked and they got out.

'Hard to imagine how it must have been, sir!'

Gently got out the sketch-plan and brooded over it, trying to reconstruct the area they had just heard talked of. The mess must have been a little distance from the hut, perhaps a matter of seventy-five yards, with the vehicle-parking to one side of it and the toilets hidden at the back. All now was bushes and dead rank grass. He walked across to it and kicked at the ground . . . traces of concrete? He advanced a little further and yes, hidden under leaves, a cracked layer of cement. He looked back towards the hut. It had been January with a black-out strictly enforced . . . Wouldn't one have expected an amorous airman to have accompanied his girlfriend when she went across there to fetch her bike?

He attempted by further burrowing to locate the entrance to the mess-building, but it was a hopeless task; nothing short of major excavation would have revealed it. He rejoined Eyke.

'No luck, sir?'

'Let's see if the hut can tell us anything.'

Eyke thrust the door aside and they entered the forlorn building. Here, time certainly hadn't stood still. Holes had rusted in the semi-circular fabric, paint was shedding from walls and roof, blackened flex hung socketless from the ceiling, and the place smelled of dung and decay. The concrete floor however was intact except for that one eye-riveting spot, at a corner adjacent to the door. There, a shallow crater was surrounded by piled shards of broken material. For the rest there was nothing in the hut but some mouldering hay bales and a rusty scythe.

'This was how you found it?'

Eyke nodded. 'It was under that pile of stuff. The concrete broke to bits as they were heaving it up. At first, all you could see was the bones of one foot.'

'They were clearly visible?'

'According to forensic it was due to a settlement of the concrete. The rest of the bones had given a bit, and the foot had tilted up through a crack.'

'When you first saw it the concrete was largely intact?'

'I wouldn't say that, sir. But not like it is now.'

Gently bent to examine the shards. In some cases the fracturing was clearly recent, in others a black deposit suggested more ancient damage. The surface of the rubble was also blackened and there were similar stains on the

45

floor round about.

'Oil . . .'

'Yes sir. That engine-cover.'

'From the signs I would say there had been more than one.'

'Perhaps this is where they dumped them, sir. And then chummie used them to cover up his work.'

'There was just one spread over the body?'

'Just the one.'

'And then others . . . piled over the grave.'

Eyke shook his head. 'Well, it must have worked, sir! Chummie has got away with it all this time.'

Gently gazed at the rubble. 'Just one problem. First, he had to break through four inches of concrete . . . And however he managed that, it would take time, and couldn't be done silently.'

'Perhaps it was bust already, sir.'

Gently shrugged. 'Perhaps! But it would still have taken a little time to prepare that grave. And if our two friends at the Old Rectory were telling the truth, neither of them had that time at their disposal.'

'So they're lying, sir.'

'That's not impossible.'

'Or one of them could have come back later.'

Gently nodded.

'Then there's that other fellow, sir!' Metfield broke in. 'The one who says he was

46

sitting in a car. He never went back inside at all, so he had all the time in the world.'

'Only—no apparent motive.'

'But we only know what they're telling us, sir!'

Gently sighed. 'And I'm afraid that's the real problem. Unluckily, we've arrived here a few years too late.'

Metfield looked crestfallen. Eyke kicked at a lump of rubble.

'I'll have them in for statements, sir,' he said. 'Get them on their own. Perhaps then they'll talk. When they haven't got the Major backing them up.'

'You could be lucky.'

'At least I can try, sir. And it's the only angle we've got.'

Gently took a last look round, but there was little more to see in the dismal Nissen hut. He went out to survey again the area, so altered, that had been the background to the crime. Bluebells were showing among the trees that clustered behind the hut, and, beyond them, was an open space where reeds were growing. He worked his way towards it. What he found was a pond, mostly overgrown, but still with some open water. A moorhen scuttled away at his approach, and a sedge-warbler scolded him from the reeds.

'He could just have chucked her in here, sir!'

Eyke had come up behind him.

47

'I was thinking of something else. The culprit had to get rid of the victim's bike.'

Eyke looked doubtful. 'If he did, sir, there can't be very much left of it now. You think we should drag for it?'

'It's up to you.'

'It's an idea, sir. But I don't think we'll bother.'

And that was all. They returned to the car, and soon were wending their way back to town. Eyke was silent as they drove, his eyes fixed on the road ahead. At last, as they turned in to park, he said:

'That Major, sir. What did you make of him?'

'Major Forrest . . . ?'

Eyke nodded. 'He runs that show, sir, no question about that. And I'm just wondering how much he knows.'

Gently puffed on the pipe he had lit. 'Probably not much more than we do! But one thing is certain about the Major.'

'Sir?'

'He'll be the last person you'll get anything out of.'

'Yes . . . I suppose so.'

'I think you can bank on it,' Gently said.

* * *

Nothing fresh had arrived at the office and Gently wasted no time in collecting his car. He

48

had done his bit—he had held Eyke's hand!—and now he owed it to Gabrielle to drop the matter there.

Would the case get anywhere? It seemed improbable, unless some stroke of luck intervened, and that seemed unlikely. At such a distance of time it would need a stroke of luck indeed ...

From the Americans they had got a possible picture of what might have happened on that evening, but it was vague and inconclusive, unsusceptible of proof. And where else could one look? To far away Bakewell? Gently shook his head as he drove. Information from that direction had been available to the police at the time. Then the 'one who knows', who had written the letter? Possibly there—or possibly not! The odds were that if the writer had possession of critical information they would have reported it directly to the police.

So ... what remained?

A confession of guilt?

But even that would need confirmation to make it acceptable: hard evidence or reliable testimony, sufficient to defy the shadow of fifty years ...

No, the odds were too long. The fate of Millicent Read would remain an unsolved mystery, a tragedy of war. In the end, it was going to wind up on the files.

'My dear, what took you so long?'

On the table lunch was waiting, one of Mrs

Jarvis's special ham salads with a sherry trifle to follow.

Over the meal, he related the morning's events and answered Gabrielle's eager questions.

'Then you have met them, all these Yanks?'

He nodded. 'For what it was worth.'

'And their ladies?'

'I met two of them.'

'Ha, what it is to be a great detective! And their hair is dyed?'

'Their hair is dyed.'

'This I could swear from the one I have seen. And, already, you are thinking?'

Gently shook his head and drank some wine.

'But,' Gabrielle said. 'From what you are telling me?'

Gently shook his head again.

'I do not know.' Gabrielle drank too. 'Before this, I am guessing what must have been the way of it. This silly girl playing fast and loose with two of those young men. And was it not so?'

'It may have been coincidental.'

'I think not.'

'She may simply have fallen victim to a rapist.'

'No, oh no. She is buried so carefully. This, my friend, was a *crime passionnel*.'

Gently made a face. 'Then too bad for Eyke! Because I doubt strongly if he will ever

50

prove it. I'm afraid it's too late in the day for that.' He shrugged. 'And perhaps that is the best way to leave it.'

Gabrielle stared. 'It is too long ago, yes?'

'Yes, too long ago.'

'This man, he shall be left to his conscience.'

'Yes.'

Gabrielle sighed. 'As you say, perhaps best.'

The coffee came, and Gently lit his pipe.

'And now,' Gabrielle said. 'We forget it. I have to ring Andy to let him know if he can expect us this afternoon. I tell him we come?'

But the visit to their friends was doomed once more to be delayed. While they were still drinking their coffee, a car pulled up on the sweep outside. They heard the bell ring. Then Mrs Jarvis appeared.

'It's one of those Yanks, Mr Gently. He's asking to have a word with you.'

'Does he give a name?'

'Says it's Osborne.'

Gently paused. 'Show him into the lounge.'

'Right you are, Mr Gently. And I found another one of these things on the mat.'

And she handed him a second such envelope as had arrived in the morning post.

Gently took it and slit it open. This time the message was briefer. In the same sprawling capitals he read:

SHE WAS GOING TO MARRY ONE OF THE YANKS

Gabrielle was at his shoulder, and he heard

her gasp.

'But . . . who could have known about that?'

It was a good question. Grimly, he folded the note back in the envelope.

Gabrielle was staring. 'And . . . this man who comes here?'

'He may just have arrived at the critical moment.'

'He was one of those?'

'He was one.'

'Oh, my dear!' Gabrielle exclaimed.

Gently finished his coffee, knocked out his pipe, and carrying the envelope, headed for the lounge. He found Osborne standing at the window, staring out at the lawn.

'You wished to see me?'

'Well—yeah! I promised Bill I'd look in . . .'

Gently handed him the envelope. 'Perhaps, first, you would like to read this.'

Looking a little puzzled, Osborne took it and unfolded the note. Then he froze, his eyes widening.

'Oh my gosh!' he said.

*   *   *

'Where—where did you get this?'

He had slumped down on the settee, with the letter still in his quivering hand. For several moments he stared at it helplessly, then threw it down on the nearby coffee-table. His eyes didn't quite meet Gently's. Gently shrugged.

'Occasionally we receive such information.'

'Yes—but who? Who knows about it?'

'It would have to be someone living in the locality.'

'But for crying out—who!'

'Someone,' Gently said, 'who appears to have inside knowledge of the situation.'

'Hell, oh hell!'

He grabbed the letter again, gazed at it savagely, his eyes measuring every word.

'You have no idea from whom it may have emanated?'

'No. Bloody no!'

'But there is no question about what it is saying?'

He tossed the letter back on the table. 'If Rita ever gets a smell of that . . . !'

'Your wife would suspect you?'

'She'd crucify me. She's always had ideas about Milly.'

'Ideas . . . that were justified?'

'Fella, have a heart!'

'But you are the one the letter refers to?'

Osborne jerked his face away, stared at a framed map that was hanging on the wall.

'Well?'

His shoulders rocked. 'Listen, Gently! You're a decent guy. If I let you in on this, you got to swear it will never get back to Rita. I know it's way back, but she can't help it, she would make our lives hell. So what do you say?'

Gently shook his head. 'I'll say this! That I won't unnecessarily disturb your wife.'

'That's a promise, fella?'

'That's a promise.'

'Then . . . I guess it's up to me to come clean.'

Nervously, he pulled out a cigarette-case and lit up: Gently pushed an ashtray towards him. He frowned, breathed smoke, seemed still uncertain how to continue. Gently said:

'You met your wife before you were posted overseas?'

Osborne nodded. 'I guess I knew her a long time before that. We were neighbours back in Boston, went to school together when we were kids. She was palsy with my sisters. It was always on, her and me. Then I was a clerk in my old man's agency, while she came in as a typist, and that lasted till the call-up.' He puffed smoke. 'Of course, I saw less of her after that.'

'But the connection was there.'

'I guess.'

'She was expecting it to continue.'

He nodded. 'I was her fella, going off to England to do his duty. We got a 48, that's all, just time to sneak home and say goodbyes. Mighty emotional, it was. I took her to a jazz joint up in town.'

'And—you were engaged.'

He frowned through his smoke. 'Nope. Not

in so many words we weren't. I guess that was the understanding, but we never made it official. I was going off and may be not coming back, I guess it didn't seem fair to tie her down.'

'It was understood, but not official.'

He puffed smoke. 'Yeah.'

'And—then?'

He stubbed the cigarette. 'You gotta understand, fella, how it was! We were flying sorties, two or three a week, and never did know if we were coming back. Kids most of us, or not much more. We were just living one day to the next. We had to live fast, there wasn't much time. The pint you were drinking could have been your last.'

Gently nodded. 'Or the dance you were dancing.'

'Yeah, that too. The chick you were smooching. Fella, you just couldn't blame them. It was then or never, and most likely the last. We lost forty-odd pilots from Toddington, and Kit's the only one I knew who survived.'

Nervously, he lit another cigarette and took several hard puffs. Grim lines were showing about his mouth as he drew in the smoke.

'So—you and Miss Read?'

'That's another story!'

'But it began as another such instant liaison?'

'No, it bloody didn't!' He puffed even harder. 'And I'm not making out that I was a saint. I had chicks, like the rest of them—behind the canteen was where we used to take them. But Milly, she wasn't one of them. Milly was a different thing again. She was an educated girl, I tried to tell you, a girl you wanted to know, to be straight with.'

'But still—a good-looker.'

'Yeah, she was that. Face and figure, she'd got the lot. When Milly walked into the mess the eye of every guy was on her. A blonde she was, long sweeping hair, and a face like an angel. And she moved like a queen.' He turned his face away. 'Hell, do I have to tell you all this!'

'In fact . . . she made a strong impression.'

'Too damned strong.'

'In your case, it was love at first sight.'

'If you want to call it that.'

'And in hers?'

Osborne puffed meanly. 'So she wasn't jumping in with both feet! Milly . . . well she wasn't like that. You had to prove yourself to Milly. First off she was real cool, like she'd been warned not to trust us guys—we were dangerous, you get me? A kinda animal you had to keep at a distance. Kit got the same notion, thought that maybe she was frigid. But I never really did believe that. Behind the ice she was all woman.'

'She liked to dance.'

'Oh, sure. I don't remember she ever sat one out. And she was great, she could swing it, as long as a guy kept his distance. Nerds like Jacko just got the elbow, but treat her right and there was no problem.'

'And you treated her right.'

'I guess. Straight off I could see she was someone special. We got to talking. She wanted to hear all about where I came from, about life in Boston. Then we talked books— she'd read a lot, and me, I took literature back at college. And art, she wasn't slow on that. And flicks and theater. She was really into things.'

'And so a relationship developed.'

He nodded, frowning. 'It took time, fella. She was holding back, I could feel it, like all the while she was weighing me up.'

'You . . . and your friend.'

'Yeah. Kit. It was him I put it down to. He was in with her too, just like me, and she was trying to make her mind up. Kit was a good-looking guy in those days. He came from Detroit, and he was into cars. Cars she was crazy about too, like at home her old man ran some sort of garage. Guess Kit was offering to teach her to drive, so he could lay his hands on a car.'

'But . . . it was you who won out.'

'Yeah.' Osborne crushed his second fag in the tray.

'You proposed to her.'

He nodded, still grinding away with the cigarette.

'And when would that have been?'

'Hell. Oh hell! Do I have to answer that?'

'Was it . . . on the night of that last dance?'

He tore the cigarette into small shreds.

* * *

Gently said: 'Did Pederson know?'

'I had to tell the bastard, didn't I?'

'On that same night?'

'No—you don't get it! I'd asked her a while before then. But she laid off, wouldn't give me an answer, said she needed time to think it over. But I was dead certain it was me she wanted, so I warned Kit to lay off.'

'How did he take it?'

'How do you think? He told me what I could do with myself!'

'He still pursued Miss Read?'

Osborne shook his head. 'Guess he knew how it would pan out. So he hung back, left me a clear field.' He studied his clenched fists. 'And on that night I got her answer.'

'She accepted you?'

'Yeah.'

'During the dance?'

'Outside, fella. It wasn't only because of the cows that she missed the last dance. We got out of there and I hugged her tight and she told me yes, she'd made her mind up, and that if I still wanted her she was ready to become a GI bride. If I still wanted her, fella! We kissed

58

the daylights out of each other. Then she said we'd have a lot to talk over, but she really did have to get back for the cows, and that she must go, and I wasn't to go with her—there'd be time for that sort of thing later on. So I kissed her some more, and let her go, and went back in, and got boozed.' He stared hard at Gently. 'And that was it. That was bloody it.'

'You saw no one.'

'Like I told you.'

'How long before your friend returned to the mess?'

'Forget it, fella! I was pie-eyed, and why would I notice a thing like that?'

'So . . . it could have been later than he says?'

'I said forget it, fella! And Kit wasn't trying to commit suicide either, when the krauts shot him down.'

Gently paused. 'Was there talk of that?'

'Oh, turn it up!' Osborne said. 'Why would there be? It wasn't till yesterday that anyone knew what happened to Milly.' His mouth was trembling. 'Some bastard,' he said. 'Some filthy sod was hanging out there. And he had to strangle her to have what he wanted, then shoved her away under the concrete. But it wasn't us, fella. Stop looking at us. More like it was some tramp who was spending the night there.'

'And that's the theory among you?'

'Get lost,' Osborne said. He fumbled out

and lit a third cigarette.

Gently said: 'Did you ever visit Miss Read at the place where she worked?'

'Elm Tree Farm,' Osborne said. 'I came here to tell you. I forgot it, but Bill Mitchell remembered.'

'And you visited her there?'

He shook his head. 'Milly wouldn't let me go hunting her there. Said I'd find her in pig-slurry up to her ears, or smelling of cow-muck and horses.'

'Was that the only reason?'

He frowned. 'Said she had a mate there who didn't like Americans, another one of those Land Girls. Said the farmer wasn't struck with us, either.'

'Did you ever meet that girl?'

'Once, in the pub. I seem to remember Milly introducing us. But she wasn't a patch on Milly, just a sturdy little chick with greasy black hair.'

'You don't remember her name.'

'Nope. And she didn't turn up at the dances.'

'You met no other friends of Miss Read?'

He shook his head. 'None that I remember.'

Gently sighed. 'Then that's all, Mr Osborne. Or at least, all for the moment. Though the police at Wolmering will be requiring you to attend and give them a written statement.'

Osborne blew smoke. He glanced nervously at the letter. 'But . . . none of this will get back to Rita?'

Gently shrugged. 'As far as is possible, what you have told me will remain confidential.'

'It just better had!' He got up. 'Guess I'll be on my way then, Gently. Guess I'll take a stroll round this village of yours till I'm feeling more settled down.'

'Try The Bell,' Gently said.

'Yeah, thanks,' Osborne said.

And Gently saw him out to his car.

CHAPTER FOUR

Elm Tree Farm: the very name suggested a distance in time, since elm trees were a feature now vanished from the Suffolk scene. A few elm hedges lingered on, a sad reminder of former glories, but the trees themselves had been wiped out by a fatal disease from across the North Sea. A sawn-off stump here and there was all that remained of elms in Suffolk.

Would even the name have survived . . . ?

In the study there were maps. Gently chose one of the largest-scale in the collection and spread it out on the desk. Marked was the 'Old Airfield', but named farms were the exception, occurring only in isolated situations to which the name would give a reference. Yet somewhere, within bicycle range . . .

Frowning, he put the map away. Did it

really matter? The odds were that tracing the farm would tell them nothing. At the time enquiries would have been made there and the information obtained given due consideration, apparently suggesting no critical pointer. What chance remained, half-a-century later?

No: the answers lay in Toddington Camp, and the truth with those who were stationed there . . . and with whom it would probably remain! Curiosity alone was directing his attention to Elm Tree Farm. Curiosity about that sad girl, whose personality was slowly becoming revealed to him . . .

He rang Eyke; and Eyke, at least, had some hard information to exchange.

'I've just had Bakewell on the phone, sir, and they've traced a relative of the victim for us.'

'A close relative?'

'Yes sir. Her brother. He's a widower, retired now. Used to run a car agency in Bakewell, and quite well-off they say. He's terribly upset, and says if it will help us, he'll arrange to come right over.'

'Did you speak to him?'

'No, I thought it best if we talked to him here. But Bakewell says he's asking about the remains, and whether he can take them back home for burial.'

Gently shrugged. 'It can probably be arranged! Anything else?'

'I'm afraid that's the lot, sir.'

Gently filled him in about the visit from Osborne and his reaction to the second, freshly arrived, anonymous note. Eyke listened eagerly, could barely contain his enthusiasm.

'So that's it, sir—the Pederson fellow! Now we've really got him on the spot.'

'It certainly suggests motive.'

'You bet it does, sir. I'll have them both in here right away.'

'Don't expect too much! The same problems remain, and even a full confession would require confirmation.'

'Don't you worry, sir. And I'll send Potty round to collect that letter from you.'

About to hang up, Gently paused. 'Did you have any luck with tracing the first one?'

'Sorry sir. All we know is they sell that sort of paper in the shop at Welbourne.'

'Any dabs?'

'Only poor ones, sir. And there's nothing much we can do about them.'

Not apart from checking those of every resident in Welbourne!

'One other thing. The farm. Does the name ring any bells with you?'

But apparently it didn't, and from Eyke's response it was, to him, a matter of little importance.

And yet . . . ?

On the shelf by the telephone lay the fat volume of the local *Yellow Pages*. Gently picked it up, flicked through to the 'F's', and located the section devoted to Farmers. Not a small section! It extended to several pages, and the alphabetised names were of the farmers, not the farms. Doggedly, he sat down with it on his knees and began to run his fingers down the columns. Farms near, farms far, halls, granges, lodges . . . and finally, yes! And in a village that was only three miles distant . . .

He underlined it, and picked up the phone.

'May I speak to a Mr Simmonds?'

'Ah, that's me. Would you be the police, then? Because I've been expecting a call from you.'

*   *   *

'I read it in the paper this morning, and Susan says she heard it on the news. Of course, we weren't around here at that time, but they told us the tale when we took this place, about the Land Girl and the Yanks, and how she disappeared. Are you sure it's her?'

'Pretty certain, Mr Simmonds.'

'Well, there isn't much we can tell you about it. We never came here till seventy-two, and someone else was here before us. An old boy called Bacon had it during the war, but he'll have pegged out years ago. After that it was a chap called Turner, and he must have been seventy when he turned it in.'

'But . . . someone told you the tale?'

'Oh, they all know about it! People don't

64

forget a thing like that.'

'Someone, perhaps, who was there at the time?'

'Shouldn't think so . . . but hold you hard!'

There was an off-phone conversation, in which a woman's voice took part. Then:

'Susan tell me old Jimmy used to work for Bacon, though whether he was here then she can't say.'

'Old Jimmy . . . ?'

'My missus'll tell you. She knows more about it than I do.'

The phone exchanged hands.

'Old Jimmy,' a woman's voice said. 'He was here when that girl went missing—getting on for ninety he'll be, now.'

'He still lives in these parts?'

'Oh yes. He still looks after himself, too. You'll find him in his cottage in the village— Croft Cottage is what it's called. And he's all there, you can take it from me. It was old Jimmy who told me the tale.'

'He remembers the event.'

'Like yesterday, he does. How she was always going around with the Yanks. And how the police came here, asking questions, and writing it all down. To tell you the truth I think he fancied her himself, and that's why he remembers it so well.' She hesitated. 'Can't the Yanks tell you anything? It says in the paper it was them who found her.'

'Perhaps you can give me his full name, Mrs

Simmonds.'

'Oh, all right! It's Jimmy Cutting.'

'And I'll find him in Croft Cottage, in your village?'

'If he isn't there you can try the pub.'

Gently scribbled it down. 'Thank you for your information, Mrs Simmonds. It may be helpful to our enquiries.'

'But don't you think it's a bit rum, those Yanks turning up there?'

Gently laid down the phone.

'You—are on to something, my dear?'

Gabrielle had been hovering in the hall nearby. She may not precisely have eavesdropped on the interview with Osborne, but perhaps had not been so far from the door of the lounge. Briefly, Gently explained. Gabrielle nodded thoughtfully.

'So, that nice American didn't waste your time! But how sad, my dear, that this thing happens when, at last, they are plighting their troth to one another. My heart goes out to him. So young, so brave. And at the time, I think, so handsome. At last she has given him her Yes and then, from that moment, she disappears. Is this not sad?'

Gently shrugged. 'At least he survived, and married his Rita!'

'Aha, a jealous lady who dyes her hair. I think he was the loser by that exchange.'

'She may have been equally good-looking, once.'

Gabrielle shook her head. 'I cannot think so. And looks are not all, my friend. It seems this poor girl was a special person, such as you men meet only once in a lifetime.'

Yes: Gently didn't contradict her; it was the character of the victim that was beginning to intrigue him.

'So,' Gabrielle said. 'You will ring the good Eyke, to tell him about the farm and this old man?'

'Perhaps—later.'

Gabrielle nodded. 'This, of course, I am expecting.' She sighed. 'I will ring Andy.'

'Tell him maybe this evening,' Gently said.

*　　　*　　　*

The road to the village of Fifield led past the gateway of Elm Tree Farm, and Gently slowed when he came to it to let his eye take in the scene. A lane, or drive, extended a quarter of a mile to a red brick building set among trees, a comfortable-looking house with outbuildings stretching to one side. The trees appeared to be oaks, but on each side of the gateway were stumps of trees that once had given the farm its name, and others were just visible, departing along each side of the lane. Fifty years since, and later, an elm avenue had guarded the approach to the farm . . . the way along which, through the black-out, with dimmed light, had cycled Millicent Read on her last journey: leaving behind her in one of those outbuildings the cows she was never to milk again. And the sad, mouldering stumps seemed to mark the great divide between that time and the present sunny Spring day.

Had she no premonition, that Land Girl, as she pedalled out to the road, no knowledge that might have warned her of the brutal fate towards which she was heading? Apparently not . . . Unconcerned by such thoughts, she had sped on her way to Toddington Camp, to the dancing, to her lover, to the blissful decision she had determined to take. And, taken it she had, before conscientiously dismissing him to return to her duties at the farm, refusing his offer to accompany her to the place where she'd left her bike . . . Had she not the smallest apprehension as she made her way towards that hut?

Shaking his head, Gently drove on to the village. Fifield was a modest place, a collection of houses spread on each side of the minor road. It possessed a pub, The Brown Cow, and a small post office shop; he made enquiries at the former, and was directed to a loke just through the village. There, in an overgrown garden, he found a thatched clay-lump cottage and, sunning himself on a bench outside it, an elderly, white-bearded man. Gently parked and approached the gate.

'Would I be speaking to Mr Cutting?'

The man pushed back the hat he was

wearing and surveyed Gently with watery eyes. He said: 'Do you're selling insurance, boy, you can forget it. I don't want none.'

'I'm not selling insurance.'

'So what are you selling?'

Gently conjured a smile. 'I'm not selling anything.'

'So who are you then?'

Gently told him: the man stared at him stolidly for several moments.

'About that Toddington business, is it?'

Gently nodded. The man still stared.

'So you'd better come in, old partner,' he said. 'And watch that gate. Thas only got one hinge.'

Gently negotiated the gate, and Cutting made room for him on the well-worn bench. A lean, angular figure in his late eighties, clad in a shabby suit of some decades back. His horny hands were clasped over a stick. There were stains on his wide-brimmed trilby. His weathered features had a ruddy tinge, and the beard straggled halfway down his chest. He tapped the flag-stones with his stick.

'Who sent you?' he said.

Gently told him.

'Might have guessed it,' he said. 'She's a beggar, that one. So what did she tell you?'

'She told me you worked at the farm during the war.'

'Ah.'

'You did work there?'

69

'Can't get out of that, can I?' Cutting said. 'Man and boy. First for old Bacon, then for the Turners, who followed him. And I've seen a few changes, I can tell you. We only had horses when I first worked there.'

'You, perhaps, remember that time well.'

'Ah. Some of those winters were the devil.'

'The war. The Land Girls coming there.'

He tapped the flags with his stick.

'Well?'

'Married one of them, didn't I?' Cutting said.

'You—married a Land Girl?'

'Ah. Poor Betty. What I lost in eighty-nine. Up there in the churchyard, she is. I took some flowers up only yesterday.'

Gently shook his head. 'I'm sorry,' he said. 'And she was at the farm with Miss Read?'

'What, Milly? No, she wasn't! Come there to take Milly's place, she did.' He stared down at the stick. 'There was all that trouble. I didn't pay any regard to Betty, at first. Your lot was always about there, trying to make out where Milly had gone. But then things went on, and Betty and me got together, and after VE Day we hitched up. And I never did have cause to regret it.'

Gently said: 'You knew Miss Read quite well?'

He tapped the stick. 'Never had a chance with her, did I? She wouldn't have looked at a bloke like me, reckon I wasn't in Milly's class.'

'But you rather liked her.'

'It wasn't no use.'

'Perhaps took her out?'

'She come to the pub once. All she could talk about was books she was reading, and how she was going to be a teacher after the war. I knew it wasn't any good. I give up trying. I'd got a little fancy bit in the village.'

'Had she other admirers?'

'Blast, yes. She could have taken her pick, Milly. But then those Yanks came here and she was off with them all the time. They'd got the dough, hadn't they, and nylon stockings, and I don't know what. Us, we were never in it, boy. You had to be here to understand.'

'Did she mention any names?'

'I'm trying to remember. Chuck, I think was one she talked about. But there were others, she wasn't particular, and all of them had got their pips up.'

'They were officers.'

'Ah. She never looked at one who wasn't.'

He shuffled his stick, laid it aside, and pulled out an ancient briar pipe. Gently offered him his pouch. Cutting accepted it, filled, lit, and took quick puffs. Gently also lit his pipe. Together, they blew smoke into the still air.

Gently said: 'Wasn't there talk of a wedding?'

'Never heard about that,' Cutting said. 'But the way she carried on it wouldn't have come as any surprise. Is that what they say?'

Gently paused, then nodded.

'It's a rum old do,' Cutting said. 'And now those Yanks come back and find her.' He shook his head. 'A rum old do.'

'Was there no suspicion at the time?'

'We just thought that she'd took off. Things like that went on in wartime, and she was in with the Yanks and all.'

'Even though she had left her possessions behind her?'

'Ah, we wondered about that. But if it was a Yank she'd cleared off with she wouldn't have bothered about a few clothes.' Cutting puffed a few times. 'Are you on to them, boy?'

Gently merely matched puff with puff.

'I reckon,' Cutting said. 'I reckon. Can't have been any other way. She got one of those blokes steamed up. That's the way these things happen.'

Gently said: 'Did you see her leave that night?'

Cutting shook his head. 'I lived down here in the village. Time I was leaving off she would have gone inside to posh up. She was wearing her fancy dress, they said, the one that only came to her knees. Of course she'd got her coat over it, but it wasn't any too warm that night.'

'Can you remember if there was a moon?'

'No, it was black as the hobs of hell. And we dusn't use a torch or nothing, do we'd have had the warden on our backs. I know I stayed indoors that night, didn't even bother going to the pub.' Cutting looked away. 'That poor little bugger. At least, my Betty died in her bed.'

Gently puffed. 'And that other Land Girl—the one who worked here with Miss Read?'

'You mean Cissy,' Cutting said. 'I can't recall what her other name was. Ah, she was all right was Cissy, I had an eye for her too. A dark-haired girl. She wasn't upshus like Milly, and she didn't go cunning round with the Yanks.'

'But they were good friends?'

'Reckon they were. She was mortal upset when Milly went missing. They give her time off to get over it—Brummagen-way, I think she come from. And she did all right in the end, did Cissy.'

'She did all right?'

Cutting nodded. 'Took up with the boss's son, didn't she? They got married soon after us.'

'The boss's son . . .'

'Young Bert. Him what never took to farming.'

'A Herbert Bacon.'

'Ah. His dad set him up in the building business after the war. Of course, while that was on he stayed at the farm so as not to get called up, but straight afterwards he set up in building. So like I say, Cissy did all right.'

73

Gently blew a careful smoke-ring. 'And—the Bacons still live in these parts?'

'W'yes. They used to be at Wolmering, but when he retired they moved to Welbourne.'

'To . . . Welbourne.'

'Got a bungalow there, that one that stand back near the church. She come round to give me a look now and then. They was at the funeral, him and her.'

For some moments, Gently was silent. Then he bent to knock out his pipe. 'Thank you,' he said. 'Thank you, Mr Cutting. What you have told me may be very useful.'

'Haven't told you much,' Cutting said. 'And that was all such a time ago, boy.' He too bent to knock out his pipe. 'Think you'll ever find out who done it, boy?'

Gently shrugged and got to his feet.

'Another world, that was,' Cutting said. 'Different people.' He sighed. 'What's this tobacco you're smoking, boy?' he asked.

*   *   *

'I thought it wouldn't take you long to find me up.'

Gently knew the bungalow quite well. Though situated in the centre of the village, it stood withdrawn, and neighbouring the churchyard. A gravel drive led to it, through well-kept gardens, and tall lime trees rose behind it. A newish Rover 100 stood on the

74

sweep: the open door of a garage revealed a Volvo.

'You'd better come in, then. Bert's inside.'

A short, dumpy lady had answered his ring. Grey-haired, with rounded fresh-complexioned features, she stared at him with suspicious, thrusting dark eyes. She was dressed in a no-nonsense blouse and skirt and sturdy shoes, perhaps intended for gardening.

'As soon as I heard I guessed they'd drag you in, and that we'd soon have you round here. Would you care for a beer?'

Gently shook his head.

'Well, come this way then. Bert's in the lounge.'

She led him to a spacious room with conservatory windows, looking out towards the church. There, seated in an armchair, was a balding man with lean, creased features and a skimpy moustache.

'Here he is, Bert—I told you we'd see him! Aren't you going to shake his hand?'

Uncertainly, the man pulled himself to his feet and extended a calloused hand. He gazed at Gently with misty grey eyes.

'You . . . want to talk to Cissy?' he quavered.

'Of course he does, stupid!' Cissy Bacon said. 'And anyone else who knew Milly. That's his job. And I worked beside her. And so did you when you couldn't get out of it.'

'But my memory. . . it isn't so good.'

'Then it's lucky he's got me.'

'I don't know . . .'

'Oh, sit yourself down again!'

'I'm sorry, Cissy . . .'

'Just leave it to me.'

She showed Gently to a chair by the window and herself took one close by. Her husband lowered himself cautiously back into his and sat gazing helplessly at the two of them. Cissy Bacon fixed her eyes on Gently.

'So—what can I tell you that you haven't heard already?'

Gently shook his head. 'Perhaps something of the character of the girl you used to work with!'

'Her character!' Cissy Bacon tossed her head. 'Well, she was twenty, and knew what she was up to. She had the looks and she wasn't wasting them, that's how I remember precious Milly.'

'She went after the men.'

'Are you kidding? Men were all that Milly lived for.'

'She was promiscuous?'

'Twice likely. She didn't tell me everything.'

'Oh, now then!' her husband muttered. 'Don't go giving him the wrong impression . . .'

'You lay off, Bert.'

'But she wasn't . . .'

'I know best what Milly was!'

Herbert Bacon hung his head.

'I ask,' Gently said. 'Because from what I've been told, Miss Read appeared to have been a

76

cultivated person. She is said to have been interested in literature, and to have had thoughts of training to be a teacher.'

'Oh well, I'll give her that!' Cissy Bacon pouted. 'There was always a pile of books in our bedroom, and she was often stuck in a corner with one. But that doesn't alter what I'm saying. It was men who came first with Milly. Perhaps it didn't show so much till the Yanks got here, but there was no holding her after that.'

'Cissy . . .!'

'Shut up, Bert!'

'But Cissy . . .'

Cissy Bacon quelled her husband with a look.

Gently said: 'The impression I was getting was that she was quite particular about her men-friends. She was fond of dancing, fond of their company, but preferred to keep them at a little distance.'

'Huh,' Cissy Bacon said.

'Wasn't that how you knew her?'

'Yes and no,' Cissy Bacon said. 'From the way she talked you might have thought different, but then I never went to those dances with her.'

'For example, she didn't stay out late.'

'Couldn't, could she, when we had to get up early for the milking.'

'She was never out all night.'

'The old man would have skinned her!'

'In fact, as far as you know, she behaved quite properly.'

Cissy Bacon's mouth compressed right. 'All right, so Milly kept her knickers on! Like I told you, she knew what she was about, and it wasn't a quick bang in the bike-shed. She'd got other ideas, had Milly, and I should think by now you know what they were.'

Gently nodded. 'And you were in her confidence?'

'She had to swank to someone, didn't she?'

'She mentioned names?'

'Of course she bloody did. That's how I know there were two of them after her.'

'Two . . . ?'

'Oh, don't act the innocent! You must have talked to those sods who found her. She had two of them on the hook, Chuck Osborne and Kit Pederson. Flight Loueys they were, flying fighters, and both of them come from good families. She got offers from the pair of them, and only didn't know which one to pick.' Cissy Bacon darted him a keen look. 'You have been talking to them, haven't you?'

Gently stared back. 'And this had gone on for some time?'

'From what she told me,' Cissy Bacon said.

'She couldn't make up her mind to either of them.'

'No.'

'Or—perhaps, whether to accept one at all?'

'If you say so.'

78

Her husband groaned. 'Oh, Cissy . . . !'

'You keep out of this!' Cissy Bacon snapped at him.

'But a nice girl like Millicent . . .'

'Shut up, Bert. I knew her better than you did.'

'She wouldn't ever . . .'

'Oh yes she would. She only hung on to work out the best deal.'

Herbert Bacon shook his bald head and stared down at his calloused hands.

Gently said: 'But there was a preference.'

'You found that out?' Cissy Bacon said. 'Yes, there was. It was Chuck she fancied, or perhaps he was offering the most. I knew he was her favourite, but she kept him hanging on, right till the night of that dance. And she more or less let on when she was sprucing herself to go there.'

'That—she was going to accept Osborne?'

Cissy Bacon nodded. ' "This is the night" is what she said. And I knew well enough what she meant. She was all of a doo-dah, like a cat that smells the cream.' The dark eyes stared into Gently's. 'And that's the size of it,' she said. 'She went there. She told him. And someone there couldn't take it.'

Gently shrugged.

'Wasn't that the way of it?'

'It's possible.'

'Oh, come on now! Nothing else makes sense. It had to be the other one or nobody.

79

She swans in there all loving and tells Chuck Osborne that he's the man, and they dance the night away, with the other bloke looking on. He's got the push, but he can't bear it. I daresay he's having a few at the bar. And then, when she goes to fetch her bike, she finds him waiting for her in there. And that's it. He's got the booze in him. If he can't have her, nobody will.' She paused for breath. 'Isn't that how you see it?'

'Oh, Cissy!' her husband wailed.

'I don't care—that's how it must have been!'

'But you shouldn't . . . you mustn't . . .'

'I'll say what I think!'

Gently said: 'Just a word of warning! You would do well to keep your suspicions to yourself. As yet we have no knowledge of who the culprit may have been, and any spreading of rumours could land you in trouble.'

Cissy Bacon's head jerked. 'But I can still think it!'

'It would be wise if you left it at that.' Gently's stare met the dark eyes firmly. 'And, just in passing, would it be you who's been sending me letters?'

The eyes were defiant. 'And if I did?'

'Oh Cissy, Cissy!' her husband gasped.

'Well, someone had to put them on the right track, Bert. And I was as close to it as anyone.'

'But . . . Cissy!'

Gently said: 'Is there anything you wish to add, Mr. Bacon?'

80

'I . . . no!'

'Oh, forget it!' Cissy Bacon said. 'I'd say it was time we had that beer. What do you say?'

But Gently merely shook his head, and rose to be shown out to his car.

CHAPTER FIVE

So, had he really got any further with the mystery of that death of so long ago? Absently, he belted himself in, and unthinkingly directed the car towards Wolmering.

A little more he knew about the times, the circumstances, the characters of the people involved, and more especially that of the victim, the blonde girl with her books, her ambitions, her appetite for life. A girl of personality . . .

Though so fond of distraction, a note of caution had always lain behind it. She had danced and flirted with the handsome airmen, but never allowed herself to be carried away. On them, on herself, she imposed a limit, and her duties at the farm were never forgotten: before the last dance was called she would fetch her bike and be on her way.

And yet, she had clearly been attracted by at least two of them, and finally . . .

Gently shook his head!

If she really had been in love with Osborne,

why had she resisted his offer for so long?

Those were not the times for protracted courtships. Each day brought the risk of its being the last. And each day as she performed her labours on the farm she would have heard the fighter-planes departing overhead. One imagined her pausing from the slurry, the pig-troughs, and staring up at the planes on their way to battle, knowing that in one of them was the man who had chosen her, and who she may have been intending to accept. So . . . why the delay? What was holding her back? Surely not the calculations Cissy Bacon suspected! No: they didn't fit with her character. Something else was the motive for her hesitation. Something else or . . . someone.

But again, Gently found himself shaking his head. If Millicent Read had truly been in love she would have turned from any thought of other pretenders. Once, they may have shared her affection with Osborne, but not then, when her heart had decided. And, if they had persisted, she would have kindly, but firmly, delivered her rejection.

A mystery, then . . . and perhaps unimportant, but buried with the victim in her grave. For a while she had resisted the promptings of her heart—it may even have been because her lover was an American? But whatever, that resistance was at last overcome, the decision taken, her word given. And still, at that important moment, she had not forgotten her appointment with the cows! In a way she had become a victim of her duty, another casualty of the war . . .

Gently sighed to himself. Life at Elm Tree Farm couldn't have been so sweet, the livestock, the horses, the daily grind of the milking parlour. Earlier, when the RAF had been at Toddington, there had probably been no dances to go to, just the pub to visit in the evenings, or a session with her books. But then the Yanks had arrived, and suddenly glamour was in the air—jazz, dances, nylon stockings, and a round-up of the local chicks! Cissy, grim Cissy, wasn't taken in—she perhaps already had an eye on Bert; but, as long as she played it cool, Milly saw no reason why she shouldn't indulge. And so the die was cast. Every dance-evening saw her on her bike. And the Yanks loved her, queued up for her hand, treated her like the belle of the ball. Two in especial, two handsome pilots . . . perhaps it wasn't surprising that she dallied so long? Detroit versus Boston: and in the end, it was Boston who won. The black-out, the rationings, the war—what did they matter to Queen Milly?

And then . . . so suddenly.

On the very night. The very moment.

Could it have been a coincidence, that, the intrusion of some chance element?

The odds were against it, though not entirely. The war had bred a few such crimes, crimes concealed by the black-out, by deserted streets, damaged buildings. A few had gone undiscovered until the removal of the debris, but never at this distance of time. If this was the answer, the trail had gone cold.

Almost unawares, he found himself in Wolmering and parking his car outside the police station: alongside a Ford Mondeo bearing hire-car markings. Eyke met him in reception.

'Bang on time, sir!' he said. 'That fellow Pederson has turned up, and we're just about to take his statement.'

* * *

'My name is Charles Christian Pederson and I reside in Detroit, Michigan, the US of A. In 1944 I was a U.S.A.A.F. pilot stationed at Toddington Camp in Britain.'

Tight-faced he sat on the chair provided for him in front of Eyke's desk, legs crossed, arms folded: ignoring the rustle of Metfield's pencil. Around 5'10" and inclining to plumpness, with receding white hair and fleshy features. His expressionless brown eyes were fixed on the desk before him.

'At the time present I am here on a visit arranged by my former CO, Major Robert Forrest, and staying with him and the rest of the party at Old Vicarage Guest House in Toddington.' He paused, let the pencil stop rustling. 'I understand that certain testimony is

84

required of me, testimony relating to my acquaintance with a person whose remains have lately been found.' He paused again, his lips taut. 'A person by the name of Millicent Read.'

It was almost comic. The careful, regulated statement was being delivered in a transatlantic accent, sounding like lines that he had been studying, perhaps under the tutelage of that same Major Forrest. Eyke was staring at him in disbelief.

'Right,' he said. 'Right, my lad. But it was a bit more than an acquaintance, wasn't it, your carryings-on with Miss Read?'

Pederson's mouth twisted. 'You expect me to tell you?'

'I want the truth, sonny. Every last bit.'

'It has to go on the record?'

'You bet.'

Pederson stared angrily at him, at Gently.

Gently said: 'You made certain admissions when the matter was discussed earlier. Are we to understand that now you wish to withdraw them?'

Pederson swore something under his breath.

'Well?'

'Goddamn the lot of you, I say!'

'And that is your answer?'

'No, it isn't! If you're going to have it, you're going to have it.'

'So . . . ?'

He jogged the chair. 'So I loved her,' he

said. 'I loved Milly. Like I never loved a dame before or since I loved that sweet girl back there. Sure, I got married after the war, a guy couldn't stay a bachelor for ever, but Milly was the one. I'd have gone through hell for her. After Milly there was just women.'

'Well, well,' Eyke said. 'Well, well. Are you getting this down, Metty?'

Pederson turned on him savagely. 'And I can guess what you guys are thinking!'

'She gave you the push, didn't she?'

'I still had a chance! Right to the end it was Chuck or me. She could have changed her mind. And this I'll swear to heaven—I never, never would have harmed Milly.'

Was it genuine? The brown eyes were explosive, and he was almost jumping off the chair. And strangely, the puffy features seemed to retire, to reveal the ghost of a younger, handsomer man. Osborne still kept his looks, it wasn't difficult to imagine him as the dashing young airman; and now one was catching a glimpse of it in the raddled countenance of Pederson. Even Eyke was a little taken aback.

'So,' he said. 'So I'm listening to you, sonny. She was your goddess in plus-fours. And right up till that last dance you thought there was still a chance for you. Is that the line?'

Pederson glared. 'How does one tell a limey like you? She wasn't just a dame, bonzo, she was real, a real person. One you could

86

respect.'

'But sexy with it.'

'She was a woman!'

'A woman who chased after the men.'

'It wasn't like that, you louse. It was them who chased after her.'

'But she didn't object to it.'

'Oh, for Chrissake! How do I get it into your head? She was a dame who kept the guys in their place—and that went for Chuck and me. She wasn't a smoocher. I never got a kiss, and I guess that went for Chuck too. The closest we got was when we danced, and she didn't hang on like the rest of the chicks.'

Eyke shook his head. 'Just a nun who liked a hop.'

'Yeah. Yeah. You can put it like that if you want to.'

'But who never missed a chance.'

'Get lost,' Pederson said. 'Get lost.'

Gently said: 'From what we have heard, she was a regular participant at your dances.'

'Then you heard wrong,' Pederson snapped. 'It was only late on she kept turning up.'

'Only late on?'

'That's what I said. First off she only came now and again. I guess she found some of the guys too pushy, guys like Jacko and a few more. But they got the message in the end, and she got the message too—we weren't all Jackos, there were some of us civilised. And after that she kept coming.'

'She liked to talk. To socialise.'

'Yeah. To get treated like she was a human being.'

'With people like yourself and your friend.'

Pederson's lips compressed tight.

Gently said: 'It was no secret between you. You were both admirers of Miss Read. And you were perhaps not alone. There must have been others equally struck by her.'

'Guess there were.'

'Some you looked on as rivals?'

He writhed in the chair. 'Hell, no! They may have fancied her rotten, but they weren't in Milly's line. In the end it was just Chuck and me, and every sod there knew it.'

Gently nodded. 'So she had to make up her mind.'

'Yeah. Yeah.'

'And we know that she did so. However painful it may be to you, Mr Pederson, she had decided that evening to accept your friend. Had you some premonition that was how it would be?'

He ground his teeth. 'I guess.'

'Perhaps—more than that?'

His shoulders hunched. 'Chuck told me to lay off. He was that damned certain.'

'He was anticipating her decision.'

Pederson simply bit his lip.

Gently said: 'So now, if you will, we will come to the evening of that dance, and every detail that you can remember.'

Pederson's eyes were staring at nothing.

*   *   *

'To begin with, did Miss Read arrive there in good time?'

For some moments he didn't seem to hear. Low sun had got round the corner of the office and was falling on the grim, set features. He made a motion with his hand, as though to brush it away.

'Sure, sure. She was dead on time.'

'Were you there to greet her—help put her bike away?'

'Nope. And Chuck wasn't there either.'

'You can be certain of that?'

'Fella, Chuck and I shared the same quarters. We were late, we'd been on some lousy lecture, we only just made it for the first dance.'

'So you found Miss Read already in the mess-hall.'

'Yeah. The band was just starting in. Milly was having a drink at the bar with Robbo and one or two of them.'

'Robbo . . .?'

'Major Forrest to you! It was him who ran these hops. And like he had an eye for Milly too, but he already had a wife back home. So Chuck grabs Milly and takes off and there isn't a chick left sitting down, which leaves me propping up the bar and getting my first drink

89

down me. I'd been warned off, remember? But I did get a dance in later.'

'With Miss Read?'

'Who do you think? And it was her who came after me.'

'She invited you?'

'Yeah.' He scowled. 'Do I have to tell you what for?'

Slowly, Gently shook his head.

'I was getting my cards,' Pederson said. 'She like told me she'd made her mind up, and that if Chuck asked her again, she was going to say yes.' His mouth puckered. 'She did her best,' he said. 'She tried to let me down light. That was her way. She was Milly. But hearing it from her just had to be wicked.'

Gently nodded. 'Did you dance with her again?'

'Mebbe once. She fixed that one too.'

'She was trying to console you.'

'Yeah. I guess. Chuck was leaning on the bar grinning at us.'

'And after that?'

'Oh heck!' He dragged his stare away from Gently's. 'Fella, I couldn't take any more, I just had to get out of that place. She was dancing with Chuck, real close, like she would never dance with me, and he'd got this stupid grin on his face, and she was smiling over his shoulder. And the other guys, they were grinning too, like they knew what it was all about. I had some drinks and tried to stick with it, but in

90

the end I had to go.'

Gently said: 'To the outside toilets.'

'Just some place! I couldn't care less. They were closest, and I went in there, and stuck a cheroot in my face.'

'Wouldn't you have done better to go back to your quarters?'

'I was going to ask that too, sir!' Eyke put in. 'This was in January, in the black-out, and it couldn't have been too cosy out there in the bogs.'

'Oh, for Chrissake!' Pederson snarled. 'Does it matter? They were the next place outside the mess. And mebbe I still couldn't believe what was happening, wasn't going to drag myself too far away.'

'Like you thought there was still a chance for you,' Eyke said.

'You go to hell!'

'Say a word in her ear after the ball.'

Pederson looked as though he could have struck him.

Gently said: 'You were alone out there?'

'Who the heck else would be there at that time of night?'

'The mess had its own toilets.'

'Right. No sod was going to disturb me out there.'

'And . . . from those toilets, could one have seen the Nissen hut?'

'No, one bloody couldn't! It was round the corner under some trees. All you could see from there was the mess.'

Gently pulled out the plan. 'You wouldn't have needed to go far. A few steps from the toilets was all it required. You are quite certain you remained in the toilets?'

'Just lay off,' Pederson snarled. 'Lay off!'

Gently shrugged. 'So how long were you out there?'

Pederson glared at the desk. 'Like I told you, while I smoked a cheroot. Mebbe twenty minutes, I don't remember.'

'So . . . it couldn't have been longer?'

'I don't remember! Fella, this was happening fifty-three years since. I could hear the band playing the last number, and after that I went back in.'

'In fact, some time after Miss Read left.'

Pederson looked daggers. 'If you say so.'

'You last saw her dancing with your friend.'

'Yeah. So now you prove different.'

Gently shook his head. 'You went back in. I believe you found your friend at the bar.'

'Like I did.' His mouth was tight. 'Guess he'd got something to celebrate, hadn't he? Me, I could have done with a drink too, but not just then, not with Chuck. He wanted me over, but I didn't hear him. I stood watching the band put their tools away. He didn't shift. I saw him put away plenty. In the end I cleared out back to the quarters.'

'His mood was celebratory.'

'I guess it was.' Had there been a slight

hesitation there?

'Did you speak about it afterwards?'

'Nope. I steered clear of Chuck the next morning.'

'And that was the day . . . ?'

He nodded. 'We weren't expecting an op that day. But word came through after breakfast and we were airborne before noon. A Heinkel got me.' He stared at the desk. 'The kraut came to shake my hand afterwards, but that was that. I never knew about Milly. The rest of the war I was out of the picture.'

'You thought she had married Osborne.'

'I thought—yeah. It wasn't till I got back I heard different.' He frowned. 'I couldn't figure it. There was only Chuck and me in the deal. If Milly had really lit out with some other guy, she couldn't have been the girl I thought her.'

'It was you and him.'

'Yeah. There was nothing else fitted.'

'No sign of a third person.'

He shook his head. 'Just Chuck and me.'

'Just Chuck and you.' Eyke was gazing at the ceiling. 'You smoking cheroots, him downing the booze. While someone out there in the Nissen hut was tucking the girlfriend under the concrete. A kind of coincidence would you call it?'

'You louse!' Pederson sprang up from the chair.

'Cool it,' Eyke said. 'Cool it. But I'm still puzzled by this phantom rapist. Need a pass, would he, to get past the guard-house?'

'There wasn't any guard-house!'

'Oh, come on,' Eyke said. 'You had military police on the gate there. Are you telling me they were looking the other way when this murderous old tramp slunk by?'

'They weren't on the gate—not there!'

'Snowdrops, wasn't that your name for them?'

'Listen—I'm telling you! They guarded the airfield, not the domestic site where we were.'

'Just . . . the airfield.'

'Yeah, the airfield—the kites, the technical site, the administration. The mess, the quarters, they were outside that, nobody gave a damn for them.'

Eyke slowly shook his head.

'It's the goddamn truth!'

Gently said: 'So an outsider could well have found his way in there.'

'Yeah—any bastard at all. Once the black-out was on, who would notice them?'

'Would you remember any instances of that?'

Pederson frowned at the desk. 'Just the chicks turning up for the dances. Out there, we didn't see many strangers. Like the camp was on a road to nowhere.'

'No men accompanied the girls?'

'Nope.'

'You saw no vagrants?'

He shook his head.

'So, though an intruder may have been to blame, it seems to have been the least likely solution.'

Pederson glared. 'If you say so!'

Gently nodded. 'We'll keep it in mind. And now, unless my colleague has any further questions, we'll have your statement prepared and let you get on your way.'

The glare didn't falter. 'Do I get a clean sheet?'

'Everyone has that, Mr. Pederson.'

'Yeah—but like tomorrow I could fly back to Detroit?'

'We would prefer you to remain here with your party.'

'Yeah, I guess. I guess.' For a moment he stood undecided.

'If you will come with me, sir,' Metfield said.

'Yeah, I guess.'

He followed Metfield from the office.

*   *   *

'So what do you reckon, sir?'

Eyke had remained silent while Gently filled and lit his pipe. Now he was regarding his senior with a slightly doubtful expression. Gently puffed till his pipe was going strongly. Then he shook his head.

'You don't think we'll get him behind bars, sir.'

'Probably not, even with a confession.'

'But he's our man, sir—you go along with that?'

But still Gently shook his head. 'All the evidence we have is circumstantial. Pederson was there, and he may have had motive, but we have nothing against him other than that.'

'He was lying, sir, about how long he was out there. And he could as well have been waiting for her in the hut. He was really cut up about getting the boot from her, and we know how these things happen.'

Gently blew smoke. 'And his friend—Osborne?'

'Osborne, sir?'

Gently nodded. 'We're accepting his word for what went on there.'

'But—he was the winner, sir! She was going to have him.'

'We have no confirmation of his story. If it were untrue that she gave her consent, we would need to look at him a little closer.'

'You mean . . . he could have followed her out there?'

'She may have had difficulty in shaking him off.'

Eyke frowned for a moment. 'No sir,' he said. 'I don't think I can go along with that. You heard what chummie has just told us, and he had it from the horse's mouth, she was going to accept Osborne. There's no getting away from that.'

Gently puffed. 'It may have been her

96

intention.'

'I can't think why chummie would lie about it, sir. Then there's that letter.'

'Yes—the letter.'

'So someone else knew about it too.'

In a few words Gently gave Eyke a resumé of his encounters with Cutting and the Bacons, of Cissy Bacon's confirmation of her workmate's probable intentions on that evening. Eyke listened intently.

'So there you are, sir! Thanks to you we've got chapter and verse. She went to that dance with her mind made up, and we have to believe what those two are telling us.'

Gently shrugged. 'I wonder!'

'Sir?'

Gently brooded over a couple of puffs. He said: 'The picture we're getting of Miss Read is of a girl who put caution foremost. At first, she went only occasionally to the dances, and always kept the men at arm's length. Then, when her acquaintance with our two friends developed, she persisted on keeping them on even terms. Finally, it seems, she chose between them, but still was loth to give pain to the one she rejected. It could have been that, at the last moment, Miss Read withdrew the consent she had given.'

Eyke stared. 'You mean . . . when they were out there?'

Gently puffed, nodded. 'Her acceptance that evening had been clearly signalled, though

97

it was only when they went outside that she gave her word. But then, at that point, caution may have returned, and she sought to withdraw it again.'

'And . . . bloody Osborne?'

'It's possible. He couldn't accept the withdrawal. He may well have pursued her to the hut, trying to persuade her to change her mind.'

'And when she wouldn't . . .'

'Then, something else was exchanged for persuasion.'

Eyke looked away, stared at the window. 'You think it's possible, sir?' he said.

Gently sighed. 'It's one more possibility. Fifty-three years down the line.'

Eyke nodded. 'And that sod Osborne seems to be making himself scarce! I couldn't get him at the guest-house. He hasn't been back there since he was at yours.'

Gently glanced at his watch. 'He intended going for a stroll, but I doubt if it was to escape surveillance. Chuck Osborne is mortally scared in case his wife gets to hear of his former intentions.'

'Could be that she'll hear of a lot more than that, sir! But I still think that Pederson is our man. Though I agree that it's twice likely that we'll never get him sitting in a cell.'

At the moment he was sitting in reception, and gave Gently a savage glare as the latter passed him by. A picture of guilt? Perhaps!

But just as likely of an innocent man enduring torments . . .

Gently returned the stare mildly, and continued on his way to his car.

*   *   *

Arriving back in Welbourne, he spotted another of the hire-cars parked by the pond near The Bell. On an intuition, he parked behind it and made his way into the pub.

'Just a half, Sid.'

His intuition was correct. Osborne was seated in a corner of the bar. He, too, had a half-pint glass in front of him, at which he was staring gloomily. Gently took his glass and joined him. Osborne barely looked up.

'You hunting for me, fella?'

Gently shook his head, and drank. He said: 'I've just come from the police station, where your friend Pederson is giving us his statement.'

At once there was alertness in Osborne's stare, but he merely took a sip from his glass.

'You are wanted there too,' Gently said. 'Just as soon as you feel able.'

'I'll get there some time, fella.'

'It would help if it was sooner rather than later.'

'Sure, sure, I get the message. I'll be on my way out of here.'

'If you would.'

He drank, and stared. 'Did you get any news out of Kit?'

'Perhaps a little,' Gently said. 'It all helps to fill in the picture.'

'He—came clean?'

Gently shrugged.

'Guess he did,' Osborne said. 'Knowing Kit. In a jam, is he, or don't I get told?'

Gently sipped his beer.

'Yeah, I don't get told,' Osborne said. 'Well, I guess it was on the cards if you don't have another prospect.'

'Tell me,' Gently said. 'Why was Miss Read so backward in accepting the offer you made her?'

'Like because I was a Yank,' Osborne said. 'Good girls and Yanks didn't mix.'

'Not—because of Pederson?'

'To hell with Kit!'

'Yet she seemed to have been sad at letting him down.'

'Yeah—Milly. She was like that. But I was her guy, first and last.'

'You, she would never have let down?'

He hesitated. 'What's that guy been telling you, fella?'

Gently shook his head. 'I'm asking you.'

'And I'm saying no—she never would have! Once Milly said yes, yes is what it was, for keeps. And on that night she said yes. And no one else was in with a chance.'

'Not your friend.'

'Not Kit. And if he says he was, he's a goddamn liar.'

Gently nodded, and drank up. Osborne stared.

'What are you getting at, fella?'

Gently said: 'Just checking facts. With a central figure in this inquiry.'

For a little longer, Osborne stared at him. Then he got to his feet, turned, and stormed out. Gently didn't intervene. Behind the bar, Sid had a grin on his face.

'You got him in the raw there, guv'nor!'

Gently simply shrugged and returned his glass.

CHAPTER SIX

Another world, with different people. That was how old Jimmy had summed it up, and how, after he had slept on it, Gently felt himself beginning to see it.

The people they were dealing with today were not those who had acted out that drama, who had felt those emotions, contracted that guilt, in a situation so alien to that of the present. A connection there had to be. The young of those days had precursed their elders of today. But, between them, lay half a century of living, of family lives, of spent careers. Could the guilt, the emotions sustained then be still attributed to these people of the present?

Outside was another sunny day, which seemed only to emphasize the point—so far they were from black-outs and the winter of that distant time!

If there was guilt, was it still worth seeking? Would justice be served by hammering it home? The daffodils by the lawn appeared to shake their heads at him, the budding hawthorn to smile its dissent.

Of course, the investigation would have to continue, but was a result so very important?

'Shall we take our walk, my dear?'

Last night, it was the Reymerstons who had come to them, old acquaintances both of them, and each with some reason to feel grateful to Gently. Needless to say the staple of conversation had been the discovery made at Toddington, the involvement of the Americans, and surprise that the crime had been so long concealed.

'Someone must have made a smashing job of it!'

'Andy, you shouldn't say things like that!'

'Well, they did. From what George is telling us, they even wrapped the stiff in an oily engine-cover. That took care of the niff, old girl, and kept her safe and sound for fifty years.'

'Andy, you're revolting. Think of that poor girl.'

'Well, her mother should have warned her to stay clear of Yanks.'

They were curious, but little more, Andy Reymerston and his wife Ruth. The case made an interesting topic of conversation but was too remote to involve any deep feeling.

With Gabrielle it was different. She had met one of the principals and her pity for him had been aroused. But even Gabrielle, after much serious contemplation, was inclined to let the matter rest. It was sad, very sad, yes? But they would just have to leave the good Eyke to get on with it. And meanwhile, with the weather staying so fine . . .

'Shall we take our walk, my dear?'

He had hesitated whether to ring Eyke to learn if Osborne had indeed presented himself, but in the end he abstained and set off with Gabrielle across the Walks. Another world, and different people . . . In the end, wasn't that what it added up to?

So they strolled over the Walks and climbed down into the little valley, where the gorse was ablaze about them and martins twittered overhead. Further on, wild plum was in bloom with cow parsley ranging below it, and—

'My dear—can it be?'

Yes! The first clear notes of a nightingale!

'Shall we go on, and come back by the road?'

It was that sort of a morning. They continued along the lane that led out of the

103

valley, past the wild plum and the commencing hawthorn. Strolling slowly, with many pauses, one at the stream that flowed under the lane, then at a bank cushioned with primroses, and another white with stitchwort.

'This is better than Kensington, yes?'

Perfume hung in the gentle air. Yellow butterflies flitted here and there and, among the martins, they spotted the first pair of swallows.

Finally they arrived at the junction with the road that would take them back again to the village.

'We could, perhaps, go a little further?'

But in the end they decided to return. Gabrielle, it appeared, wished to visit the shop, and Gently wanted a word with the gardener.

However, they hadn't got far when a passing car braked suddenly in front of them, and coming up with it, Gently found himself staring in at Mrs Bacon. She reached over to drop the window.

'Are you busy this morning?'

What did one say? Reluctantly, Gently introduced her to Gabrielle. Gabrielle gazed at her with interest.

'And you actually knew that poor young woman?'

'Knew her, worked with her, shared the same room for eighteen months.'

'And you went to these dances also?'

'Good lord no! I had more sense.'

'But you knew of these men?'

'They were all she talked about. And I met them once or twice in the pub. I've seen them since around the village, and they've changed a bit, I can tell you.'

'But then . . . they were handsome young men?'

Cissy Bacon snorted. 'Milly seemed to think so!'

'One I have met,' Gabrielle said. 'This one she shall marry. I am thinking that once he was a good-looking man.'

'Chuck Osborne?' Cissy Bacon said. 'Well, perhaps.'

'You think she makes the right choice?'

'You could say that. Kit Pederson . . . well, I don't know!'

'You did not like him?'

'I didn't like any of them. I'd found my man, and he wasn't a Yank.'

'How sad,' Gabrielle said. 'How sad. And then these same men come back to find this.'

'Someone would have done,' Cissy Bacon said. 'Sooner or later. And it could be that the Yanks knew best where to look.'

'You are saying . . . ?'

'Oh no, I wouldn't dare! Your husband has warned me against shooting my mouth off.'

'But . . . ?'

Cissy Bacon shook her greying locks. 'Let's leave it there, shall we?'

Gently cleared his throat. He said: 'Was

there something you wished to tell me?'

'Well—!' Cissy Bacon patted the steering wheel. 'If I could have a word with you on my own.'

'Relating to the inquiry?'

She nodded. 'Something I'd rather Bert wasn't in on. You've seen what he's like. I'd soonest I didn't have to tell you this in front of him.'

Gently stared at her. He said: 'I think you should understand that my role in this affair is unofficial. If you have information to communicate it should be to the officer i/c at Wolmering.'

'But it's you I want to tell—I mean, everyone knows!'

Gently shrugged. 'Then as long as you understand!'

'Listen,' she said. 'I won't interrupt your walk. But you'll find me in the tea-room back in the village. It'll be empty at this time of day, so we can have our chat there. All right with you?' And she wound up the window and let in her clutch.

'Well, that lady has a nerve!'—Gabrielle stared after the departing car. 'I think you will ignore her, yes? Her tales she can tell to the good Eyke.'

'Perhaps I'd better humour her,' Gently smiled. 'Or we may be getting some more of those enigmatic letters.'

'Ha. It was her who sends them?'

106

'Her husband would prefer her to be a little more discreet.'

'Her husband—yes.' Gabrielle looked knowing. 'And what is this she shall tell you, that he musn't hear? My friend, I begin to think that, after all, she was not such an enemy to those Yanks.'

Gently chuckled. 'You think she fancied them?'

'Aha. And perhaps one in particular.'

'Her friend's suitor?'

'Why not? At least, she thinks her friend made the right choice.'

Gently shook his head, smiling.

'Then, perhaps the other one,' Gabrielle said. 'And then, oh dear! She sees him back here in Welbourne, and it may be when she has her husband on her arm. What shall she do? Already, in those days, her husband had suspicions. So, if there are tales that need to be told, it must not be while he is present. You think it may be so?'

'It's a possibility!'

'I do not like that lady,' Gabrielle said. 'I think she would stop at nothing. You must be prepared for some lies, my friend.'

'I'll heed your warning,' Gently smiled.

'I am not sure you should be left alone with her.'

They resumed their walk, ahead the village, to the right a distant prospect of Heatherings, its dormered windows standing high above

107

the Walks and neighbouring woodland. The flowery verges and hedgerows seemed alive with small birds, while their nightingale must have followed them since they heard him again in a grove they were passing.

'Confound that lady!'

'I'll hand her on to Eyke.'

As they entered the village, Gabrielle hesitated.

'Perhaps I come too?'

'Better not. She will probably dry up if you are present.'

'I could drink my coffee in a corner.'

But Gently shook his head.

'So,' Gabrielle said. 'Watch your step, George Gently. Or your wife will come and root you out.'

* * *

The tea-room was opposite the shop and approached through a little shrubby garden. As Cissy Bacon had forecast, it was empty of customers, and he found her seated alone in a room at the back.

'Just a coffee . . .'

He took his seat at her table, by a window that overlooked the pond. She acknowledged his presence with a flickering smile, but said nothing till the waitress who brought his cup had retired to the counter. Then she fixed him with her dark eyes.

'Your wife. She's French, isn't she?'

'Gabrielle is a native of Rouen.'

'Then she probably understands these things. We'll have to have a yarn together one day.'

Gently said nothing. She looked out at the ducks.

'My husband,' she said, and stopped.

'Your husband?'

She nodded. 'Yes.' Still she was looking at the ducks. 'He's never going to tell you this himself, but I think you ought to know.'

'To know what?'

'In so many words! During the war he was doing jobs for Works and Bricks—that's what they called the civvy workers who looked after maintenance on the camp. Officially he was doing farm work or they would have called him up, but in fact he spent most of his time on jobs for the firm where he'd been apprenticed. Do you get me?'

Gently sat very still.

'He worked at the camp, that's what I'm trying to tell you! He got to know the blokes there. He knew some of those who are over here now.' She paused, staring hard at the ducks. 'And this is what he's never going to tell you. He was there that night when Milly went missing. They'd got him on overtime, doing a job he couldn't very well have done during the day.'

'He was . . . there?'

109

She was nodding at the ducks. 'And not so very far away! He was fixing a mirror in the women's toilets, in the block a few yards from the officer's mess.'

*   *   *

Nervously, she drank from her cup, her eyes still avoiding Gently's. Her rounded features were without expression, her sturdy body stiff in the chair. In a moment she was fiddling in her bag and producing a cigarette. She lit it with a lighter and breathed smoke towards the window.

Gently said: 'Your husband told you of this?'

She shook her head. 'We all knew it at the time. Bert didn't make any secret of it, he could hear the dance going on in the mess. He had to be there then, because the toilets were in use during the day. They had civvy women working in the cookhouse, and that was the toilet for them.'

'He was there all the evening?'

'Yes, till late. He had a shelf to put up as well as the mirror.'

'Till after the dance ended?'

'Yes, that's what he said. But he couldn't have seen what was going on round the front.'

'He didn't see Miss Read.'

'No. And he wasn't where he could see that hut. He kept his own bike with him of course,

110

on account of having his tool-box on it.'

'So—he was there, but had nothing to report.'

The cigarette jigged. 'Yes. Or that's what he thought, at the time.'

Gently regarded her. 'But . . . since?'

'Since then—well, we know what happened to her, don't we?' She took a few quick whiffs. 'We talked it over,' she said. 'Bert and me. I mean, we both knew Milly and what was happening at that time. She was going to have Chuck, she had made her mind up, she was going to tell him at the dance, and that meant she was turning down Kit, there's no two ways about that. At the time she just seemed to have vanished, to have got on her bike and done a bunk. It looked a bit suspicious, I'll give you that, but the police weren't too much concerned. There was a war on and they were short of men, and odd things like that went on at the time.'

'It raised no concern that she'd abandoned her possessions?'

'Her possessions!' Cissy Bacon sniffed. 'Her working gear and a load of old books—any money she'd taken with her.'

'Did she have money?'

'She was never short. She used to get postal orders from home. So if she had decided to bale out, she probably had the means to do it.'

Gently nodded. 'Carry on.'

Cissy Bacon breathed smoke. 'It was Bert,'

she said. 'He couldn't get over it. That he'd been around there when it was going on. I kept after him like you would, trying to get him to remember every detail, I was sure there must be something. But you know Bert.' She sighed.

Gently studied her. 'But—at last—he came across?'

She nodded. 'I got it out of him. At one point he'd gone outside to fetch a tool from his box.'

'And?'

'Saw a bloke,' she said. 'A Yank. One of them. Saw him come out of the other toilet and slink off round the back of the mess.'

Gently stared very hard. 'Did he see him return again?'

'No, of course he sodding didn't! He just collected the tool he was after and went back in, to get on with the job.'

'And this he failed to report to the police?'

'Don't be daft!' Cissy Bacon said. 'It didn't mean anything then, we didn't know what had happened to Milly.'

'But—now you know?'

She shook her head. 'They won't get anything out of Bert. That's why I'm telling you myself, because I thought you ought to know.'

'The man was an American.'

She eyed the ducks.

'And would this American have a name?'

'I dragged it out of him,' she said.

'So?'

'Who the hell do you think? It was Pederson.'

* * *

Gently drank some coffee. Cissy Bacon flicked ash from her cigarette. On the pond, the ducks had made a sudden rush for the bank, where someone was feeding them from a bag. They quacked excitedly, chasing each other, one with a crust held high in its beak.

Gently said: 'Were you engaged to your husband at the time when this was going on?'

The dark eyes met his suspiciously. 'Not officially we weren't, but it was understood.'

'But you were still a free agent.'

'I don't know what you mean.'

'I'm trying to understand,' Gently said. 'By your own account you tried to ignore the presence of the Americans.'

'So what if I did.'

Gently shrugged. 'It makes you a little unusual!' he said. 'For most of the local girls, the coming of the Yanks was a bright spot in the gloom of those times. They brought jazz and nylon stockings and lively nights in the pubs, and their appearance and their accents were those of the idols of the screen. Could you have been so completely indifferent to them?'

There was anger in the eyes. 'What are you

113

getting at?'

'Just a thought,' Gently said. 'Pederson. You would have met him a few times. When he was not the sour old veteran he is today.'

'So flaming what!'

'I'm wondering,' Gently said. 'In the early days he was perhaps more available, more ready to spread it about, to chance his arm with the local talent. There could have been an earlier liaison, one that seemed to have possibilities. But then, as time went on, it was dropped, and all his attention was given to Miss Read. Wouldn't that have been possible?'

'You bastard!' she said. 'Are you saying I had an affair with Pederson?'

'An affair that went wrong,' Gently said. 'An affair that left you hating him. And now he presents a target for revenge, and you are doing your best to point us towards him.'

'But it isn't true, you sod!'

'Then why write those letters?'

'Because—because someone had to tell you. But it isn't true. There was never any affair with him. I didn't run round with him or any other Yank.'

'No nylon stockings, nights at the pub?'

'Bloody no! I had more self-respect.'

'We can always ask Pederson.'

'Then go on—ask him. Unless he's a liar, he'll tell you the same.'

Gently shook his head. 'So, out of pure love of justice, you've been trying to push us

114

towards Pederson. And, when we didn't seem to be picking it up, you've brought us this tale about what your husband saw.'

'It isn't a tale, you beast. It's what happened!'

'Then why hasn't your husband reported it himself?'

'Because—because!' She stared at him wildly. 'I told you, Bert doesn't want to have anything to do with it. Can't you understand that?'

'I'm trying,' Gently said.

'He thinks it was all too long ago, and he doesn't want to stir things up.'

'Unlike yourself.'

'Yes, you sod! And you should be grateful to me for telling you. If Bert knew, he would slag me off. It was bad enough me sending those letters.' She stubbed her cigarette. 'I'm going,' she said. 'I've had enough for one morning. I've tried, I've done my best to help you, and if that isn't good enough, then too bad.'

'Wait,' Gently said.

'What for?'

'Because,' Gently said. 'I'm coming with you. It isn't enough that you should tell me this, I shall need to hear it from your husband.'

'But you can't! He'll give me hell.'

'I'm sorry about that,' Gently said.

'And he'll probably deny every part of it!'

Deliberately, Gently finished his coffee.

'Oh, bloody come then,' Cissy Bacon said.

115

'And see where it gets you—I've done my best!'

Herbert Bacon was watering a seedbed when they arrived back at the bungalow, a straw hat covering his balding head and gardening gloves his calloused hands.

A shrunken, rather frail figure, dressed in a suit that had seen better times: a man nearing his fourscore and resigned to these latter days. He looked round and stood staring as they approached.

'Aren't you the policeman who was here yesterday . . . ?'

'Oh go on, Bert,' his wife said. 'You know very well who he is!'

'My eyes . . . they're not so good.' He gazed at Gently. 'You wanted me?'

'You'll soon hear what he wants,' Cissy Bacon said. 'Now let's go in. We needn't stand out here.'

Shaking his head, he put down the watering-can, peeled off his gloves and arranged them upon it. In the hall he paused to hang up his hat before ambling through to the lounge and taking his chair by the window.

'Sit down, do,' Cissy Bacon said to Gently. 'If you stay standing up you'll make him nervous.'

She plumped down herself on a chair opposite her husband: perhaps the one that Gently would have chosen. She stared keenly at her husband.

116

'Now then, Bert! I ran into this gentleman this morning, and for better or worse I thought I should tell him what we were talking about last night.'

'You told him . . . ?'

'Yes, I told him. And it's no good your carrying on. He as much as called me a liar, and wants to hear it from your own mouth. You get it?'

'Yes . . . but Cissy!'

'Never mind that! He wants you to tell him. How you were doing that job in the toilets, and what you saw when you went out to your tool-box.'

'But Cissy, after all this time . . .'

'Do you want him to call your wife a liar?'

He shook his head and stared at his hands.

'Oh, get on with it!' Cissy Bacon said.

Gently said: 'Your wife tells me that you were working on the campsite on the night that Miss Read disappeared, that you were installing a shelf and a mirror in the women's toilets. Do you have a clear memory of that?'

After a pause, the balding head nodded. 'I remember that . . . the shelf and the mirror.'

'And it was on that particular night?'

'I can't be certain . . . my memory . . .'

'Oh Bert, how can you!' Cissy Bacon broke in. 'You were certain enough about it last night.'

He stared at his hands. 'It may have been that night. It was somewhere around then.

Perhaps . . .'

'You heard the band in the mess, you told me!'

'Yes . . . the band.'

'It was that night.'

Herbert Bacon said nothing.

'We'll accept it was on that night,' Gently said. 'You were working in the women's side of the toilet block that stood to the rear of the officer's mess. How long would you have been there?'

'Oh . . . till late.'

'Before the dance began?'

After a pause, he nodded.

'And till after it ended?'

'I heard the music stop . . . I was there a bit after that.'

'And you had occasion to go to your tool-box?'

'It was strapped to my bike . . . outside.' He hesitated. 'My plane, I think it was. I'd have been putting up the shelf.'

'You put the shelf up after the mirror.'

'Yes. The mirror didn't take very long. But the shelf I had to make.'

'So . . . it was later on when you went outside.'

'I may have been out to my box before . . .'

'But it was on this occasion, late on, when you saw the man emerge from the other toilets.'

His hands moved. 'I couldn't swear to it,

that . . .'

Really, as evidence, was it worth proceeding with? The whole impression that Herbert Bacon gave was of a man drifting into senile bemusement. His hazy eyes remained fixed on his hands, he hesitated before answering any question. His pale, lined features appeared incapable of expression. You had the feeling that he was somewhere a long way off, and responding at the very edge of consciousness.

Gently said: 'Did you or didn't you see such a man?'

'I saw . . . yes, I think.'

'Though it was a dark night, with a black-out?'

'Yes . . . the window. The curtains.'

'The curtains?'

'They weren't proper ones, not like they should have been. They let a little light through, and I could see him when he passed in front of them.'

'You heard someone come out?'

'I . . . heard something. That's why I looked across there. It was the window of the kitchen, the kitchen at the back of the mess.'

'A man.'

'Yes, a man.'

'An American serviceman.'

'I could see the uniform.'

'And proceeding which way?'

The hands moved. 'Round the mess . . . in that direction.'

119

'In the direction of the hut where people left their bikes?'

He paused several seconds, then tremulously nodded.

'From where you were, could you have seen that hut?'

'No. It was right round the mess, on the far side.' He made an effort to pull himself together, and briefly the moist eyes searched out Gently's. He said: 'You can't go on like this! He could have gone anywhere, that bloke. And it could have been a different night, I was often there late on a job.'

'Rubbish!' Cissy Bacon stormed. 'It was that night, and you know it was, Bert. You told me so. You remember all right. Stop trying to make me out a liar.'

'But it was so long ago . . .'

Her eyes savaged him. His gaze dropped again to his hands.

Gently said: 'The man you saw was a serviceman. Can you be any more precise than that?'

'Of course he can,' Cissy Bacon snapped. 'At least he could when he was talking to me.'

'A man you could identify?'

'Tell him, Bert.'

Herbert Bacon sank his head. 'I told her it could have been—but I can't be certain! I told her it could have been . . .'

'Yes?'

'The one they called Kit.'

'Kit Pederson?'

He nodded. 'But I can't be certain. I couldn't swear to it!'

His wife's eyes blazed at him.

'You would have known this man by sight?' Gently said.

'Of course he flaming would!' Cissy Bacon broke in. 'We used to see him and the others at the pub. I remember him buying Bert a drink one night.'

'I didn't know him well, Cissy . . .'

'But you knew him.'

'It could have been any one of them out there . . .'

'So why did you tell me it was Kit?'

'You just kept on at me. I had to tell you someone!'

'Liar!'

'Here, here!' Gently said. 'Let's try to keep this in line. You knew Pederson by sight, Mr. Bacon, and it occurred to you that he might have been the man you saw.'

Herbert Bacon studied his hands. 'No,' he said. 'It wouldn't be fair. I never knew who it was. I couldn't see much more than a shadow, just enough to know it was a Yank.'

'But it might have been Pederson?'

'It . . . could have been any one of them.'

'Just . . . an unknown serviceman.'

He shook his head. 'She never should have told you,' he said. 'After all this time, can it really matter? It's too long ago, whoever it

121

was. And my memory . . . it's not of the best.'

Gently stared at him. 'You can't swear to an identity.'

'No, I can't. Whatever Cissy tells you.'

'Or perhaps—you won't?'

He hung his head. 'It's too long ago,' he said. 'Too long.'

Slowly Gently nodded.

'Oh, he's impossible!' Cissy Bacon said. 'But you know what you know. You're not daft. If you were guessing who it was before, you can't be guessing after this.' She eyed Gently. 'How far am I out?'

Gently stared back at her, and shrugged. He said: 'Your husband may be right.'

'Oh, men,' Cissy Bacon said. 'Men!'

CHAPTER SEVEN

'So, you were not kidnapped!'

Lunch was on the table when he got back to Heatherings, but first he had to put through a call to a discouraged-sounding Eyke. Yes, Osborne had been to the police station, and yes he had given them his statement—but where did that leave them? Suspicion they might have, but nothing that would ever get to court. Proof, hard evidence lay buried in the past, and there it was likely to remain . . .

And had Gently anything better to offer?

Eyke heard him out with respect, perhaps at first with a trace of excitement, but rapidly losing it again.

'You think it's just his missus trying to egg him on—she's got her knife into Pederson?'

That certainly summed up the impression he had brought away from the encounter.

'I think Bacon may have seen Pederson while not being positive that it was him. Whether or not he refuses to swear to it, and pleads his memory is not to be relied on.'

'So it still gets us nowhere, sir.'

'At best it would only offer confirmation.'

'Do you reckon it's worth us getting his statement?'

'I think you may have difficulty with that.'

So, apparently, did Eyke; but he promised to think about it, and on that note Gently hung up.

'This lady, she is worse than I thought!' Shamelessly Gabrielle had listened to the call. 'She has reasons, I am sure of this, for wanting to put the blame on that man.'

'It did occur to me,' Gently smiled.

'Something that happened in the old days, yes—the way I was telling you?'

'It would explain her attitude. Why, as Eyke put it, she has her knife in him.'

'Her knife in him—yes.' Gabrielle nodded. 'And did you put this to the lady?'

'She, of course, vehemently denies having had any connection with Pederson.'

'And this you are believing?'

'Perhaps not quite!'

'Me, I am not believing at all,' Gabrielle said. 'This knife, it is such a sharp one. Good reason there must be for her hating that man, and if not this, what else shall it be? Can you think of some other?'

Gently shook his head.

'So it is settled,' Gabrielle said. 'She was crossed in love, and because of this you shall not believe any word she says. And I, I shall dislike her as much as before. And here is Mrs Jarvis come to serve the lunch.'

The subject was dropped, but it left a question: could there have been another reason for Cissy Bacon's behaviour? She had wasted no time in getting her oar in, the news had scarcely broken when she was scribbling that letter. Something had been triggered, deep in her past, that had urged her to immediate action. A disappointment in love was the obvious conclusion, but did that explain such an instant reaction?

During lunch he was silent, brooding over it. How much did Cissy Bacon and her husband know? Clearly, their information arose from the latter, and just as clearly he intended to withhold it. It wouldn't be fair, he had said at one point, too many years had intervened. So—what had he seen? Pederson entering the hut? Had curiosity led to him following the airman? And was it only now, with the discovery of the remains, that he realised the importance of what he had seen that night? Perhaps . . . and perhaps he also reflected that, next day, Pederson had paid a price for his crime. He had been shot down: it was punishment sufficient. Fifty-three years later it wouldn't be fair . . .

If such was the case then one thing was certain—he hadn't passed on all he knew to Cissy! His account to her must surely have stopped short at his sighting of Pederson leaving the toilets. More she might suspect, but he wouldn't oblige her, or she would certainly have revealed it. And as it stood, it offered no proof absolute that Pederson was the guilty party. Was it enough, in itself, to explain her attitude of aggression?

'You are thinking, my dear?'

He sighed. 'You are right. We should leave it to the good Eyke!'

'That wicked lady, I think she upsets you— poof! You must put her out of your head.'

'I think you are right.'

'Yes, I say. Or your wife may begin to feel jealous. Shall we drive out this afternoon?'

He nodded. 'We can take a trip down the coast.'

But alas and alack, once more their plans were to suffer intervention. Mrs Jarvis had barely brought in the coffee when the phone began to ring.

'It's for you, Mr Gently.'

He took the phone.

'Is that you, Gently?'—the voice was that of Major Forrest. 'Look, Gently, I'll regard it as a favour if you call in this afternoon. Can you make it?'

Gently paused. 'Have you something to tell me?' he said.

'I'd like a word, let's put it that way. And you're the guy I want it with.'

'Any information should go to Wolmering HQ.'

'Yeah, yeah. We've had those guys around. But you're the boss-man, I guess, and it's you I want a talk with. O.K. ?'

He shrugged, and hung up.

'It was those Americans?' Gabrielle asked.

Gently explained.

'Aha,' Gabrielle said. 'Then this time, my friend, you shall take me too.'

'You wish to come?'

She nodded. 'I will talk to those ladies. Perhaps about their hair.'

*   *   *

'I thought we could talk in the garden, Gently. I've had them set up the booze out there.'

If Forrest was surprised that Gently had brought his wife with him, he gave only a modest indication of it. Politely, he suffered an introduction and took Gabrielle's extended hand; then, after a moment's hesitation, he led

126

them inside and through to the lounge.

'The guys are mostly out but the ladies are still around.'

Three of them in fact: his wife, Lucille, one called Beth, and Rita Osborne. They rose to be suitably introduced to Mrs Gently, who knew, at a glance, that each one of the three dyed her hair.

'O.K. if we leave you girls together?'

Sun was shining warmly on the lawn by the beeches. There stood a table and two chairs, and on the table glasses and bottles of beer. Deftly, Forrest uncapped the bottles and poured their contents into the glasses. Then he motioned Gently to be seated and drew up a chair alongside him.

'I got a taste for this stuff during the war . . . but I guess we aren't here to talk about that!' He drank, then looked long at Gently. 'O.K.,' he said. 'Tell me. I can take it.'

Gently drank too. 'Tell you what?'

Forrest shook his grey head. 'Just give it to me straight! I know which way the balls are rolling. I've talked to Chuck, talked to Kit, and had words with that guy who handles the business. And what I want to hear from you, Gently, is whether it's time for me to be getting in touch with the Embassy. Because this we won't take lying down, no sir. Six veterans came here, and six are going back.'

'You're asking me . . . ?'

'Darned right I am! When are you guys

aiming to make a move?'

'You mean—an arrest?'

'What else? Is it going to be today, or some time next week?'

Slowly, Gently drank. 'No arrest is planned,' he said.

'Don't give me that!'

'It's true. The investigation is still proceeding.'

Forrest's hawk-like features jerked. 'Listen, sunbeam! I wasn't born yesterday. There's been a case building up here ever since Bill and Jacko found those bones. You've taken statements, you've been through the drill, and we know damn well who you've got your eye on. So don't go slagging me off with fudge about investigations proceeding.'

Gently shook his head. 'That's all I can tell you!'

'You mean, I don't get to know.'

'I mean that's how the matter stands. At the moment, we know of no grounds for bringing a charge.'

'At—the moment?'

Gently resisted a shrug and took another pull from his glass.

Forrest stared at him with narrowed eyes, then also took a quick sip.

Across at the house, through french windows, they could see the ladies sitting in a close group, while from somewhere at the back a maid had emerged to shake out a table-cloth.

She gave a look in their direction before retiring into the house.

Overhead, a dove was crooning; and they could hear the distant moan of a tractor.

Forrest drank again. He said:

'See here, Gently. You're building a case against one of my men. Maybe there's reasons that I don't know about, but from what I do know the guy's neck is sticking out. His pal was getting away with the girl, and he couldn't even bear to watch it going on. I know, because I was there. And I was there when he was shot down. And I'm going to tell you he was asking for it, he took no evasive action at all.'

'He let it happen?'

'Yeah. He was a sitting duck for the jerry. Just kept flying straight and level while he was blasted out of the sky. And he was one of my best pilots who knew the game from A to Zee. But not that day. Like he wanted it to happen. Like he wanted to have done with life.'

'Because his conscience . . .'

'Goddamn it, no! Because he'd lost out with that girl. And I'm blaming myself for that, Gently, I should never have taken him on that op. I knew what state of mind he was in, and him a kid, not much over twenty. But the order came through, it was a rush job, and they called for every kite we could muster.' He looked away. 'I had to write to his parents, tried to let on he could have survived. Guess you can imagine the relief I felt when we got to

129

know that he had made it.'

Gently nodded. 'And you can be certain . . . ?'

'Yeah. Like I'm sitting here. He couldn't have done that, not Kit, not however much she'd let him down.'

'Not . . . in that first moment of despair.'

'Lay off it, fella. Lay off it!'

'Though perhaps in drink?'

He ground his teeth, and stared at the house.

Gently drank. Through the french windows they could see the maid pouring cups of coffee, and one of the ladies lighting a cigarette. As though stirred by the sight, Forrest pulled out and lit a cigar. He sat a moment puffing, then he sighed.

'Don't get it wrong,' he said. 'Kit wasn't boozed that night. He was dancing like the others, just had a nip or two now and then. He danced with the girl, you know that?'

'It was in his statement,' Gently said.

'Yeah, well,' Forrest frowned. He took a pull from his glass.

Gently said: 'You were present all the evening?'

Forrest merely puffed smoke.

'I was wondering,' Gently said. 'Whether you remember at what point Pederson absented himself from the mess.'

Forrest drank some more. 'Guess it was late on,' he said.

'About how late?'

130

'Maybe a couple of dances still to go.'

'You saw him leave?'

He nodded. 'Like I was keeping an eye on him,' he said. 'We could all see what was going on and I didn't want there to be trouble. I was in a mind to have a word with the guy, but he must have guessed it, and stayed clear. So when he stalked out it was a relief, and I just hoped we wouldn't see him again.'

'He left by the main doors?'

'Sure. He marched across the floor through the dancers, then lugged the curtains aside and slammed the door after him.'

'He was in a rage.'

'Yeah—I guess. But that was with Chuck and not the girl. I thought he turned off towards the quarters, but seemed he was heading for those outside bogs.'

Gently paused. He said: 'Perhaps you can remember something else. I'm given to understand that some work was in progress in the women's side of the toilets. Would that have been the case?'

Forrest frowned at him. 'Have a heart, fella!' he said. 'The toilets belonged to Admin, they were nothing to do with me.'

'You wouldn't have noticed?'

'No.'

'It involved the installation of a shelf and a mirror.'

He hung on a moment, puffing. 'And this was going on the night of the dance?'

'So I'm informed.'

'There were guys around there?'

'A single workman. A civilian.'

Forrest's stare was tight. 'And you've talked to this guy—he saw Kit?'

Gently nodded.

'Hell,' Forrest said. 'Hell.' He puffed hard. 'So what is he telling you?'

'Just that he saw him.'

'No more than that?'

Gently drank. 'A very little more. He claims to have seen an airman who may have been Pederson leave the toilets and depart in the direction of the Nissen hut.'

Forrest's eyes were two slits. 'Who—may have been?'

'In the black-out he couldn't be certain. He saw him as a shadow passing in front of a window. But in the circumstances it could not well have been anyone else.'

'Yeah—yeah.' Forrest flicked the cigar. 'But this guy didn't actually see him go into the hut?'

Gently shook his head. 'He had no reason to follow him. He fetched a tool he had come out for and returned into the toilets.'

'So that's it, fella!'

Gently stared at him.

'Kit—he was on his way back to the mess. Like he decided to go round that way, and that's all you can make out of that.'

Gently drank and said nothing. Forrest

flicked ash and took several puffs. The invisible tractor, which had fallen silent for some minutes, now began its busy moaning again. Forrest frowned at nothing.

'This guy. You got a sworn statement from him, have you?'

'Not . . . yet.'

'How d'you mean, not yet?'

Gently shrugged. 'When I spoke to him this morning he appeared reluctant to proceed with one. He understood that his testimony was critical but felt it would be unfair to maintain it at this distance of time. He alleged uncertainty about the man he saw, and even whether it was that particular night.'

Forrest breathed smoke. 'But you think he'll come clean?'

After a moment Gently nodded. 'He's under pressure. He made the admission to his wife. It was she who brought the matter to my attention.'

'You think she'll keep needling him.'

'Yes.' Gently looked towards the moan of the tractor. 'She knew the victim. She was Millicent Read's workmate. She saw her set off to the dance that evening. She was aware of the whole situation and especially of the part that Pederson played in it.'

'You mean—she's out to get the poor bastard?'

'I'm afraid there's little question about that.'

Forrest kept staring. 'You say she was a

133

workmate—another one of those babes in plus-fours?'

Gently hesitated. 'Did you know her?'

'Guess I may have done,' Forrest said. 'A stumpy little dark-haired chick who used to hang around with Milly. I must have seen her in the pub a few times. Yeah, sure. She looked like a doll who might bear a grudge.'

'Was she ever at the dances?'

'I don't recall that. But she'd have looked different dressed up.'

'Did you ever see her with Pederson?'

'Well, just around.' His eyes narrowed. 'You think you're on to something there?'

'It . . . might explain her hostility.'

'It sure might' Forrest chewed his cigar. 'And now she's got a card in that husband of hers.' He chewed some more. 'The poor devil,' he said. 'Kit. He's got everything against him. But he isn't dead yet, fella, you don't have a case there. And I'm saying it who has sat on a few court martials.'

Gently shrugged, drank. 'You saw him stalk out of the mess,' he said. 'Later he came back in. Can you remember when that was?'

Forrest spat a shred of cigar. 'Maybe. And he wouldn't have had time to bury any bodies.'

'So?'

'After the last dance,' Forrest said. 'Straight after. And he banged the door that time too, so like everyone there could swear to it.'

'He hadn't cooled down.'

134

'I guess not.'

'There was no trouble between him and Osborne.'

Forrest spat again. 'I was waiting for it. But no, there wasn't any trouble. Kit gave him some dirty looks but then he tramped across to watch the band put their instruments away. I had my eye on him, you bet, and maybe that made him careful. He hung on there for maybe ten minutes and then slunk off back to quarters.'

'You can be sure of that.'

'Yeah, sure. Some of the other guys were leaving with him.'

'Not—Osborne.'

'No. Not Chuck. Chuck was still ladling it down at the bar.'

'Celebrating his engagement.'

'I guess. In the end, I had to warn him to pack it in.' Forrest was frowning. 'You know the tale. Milly left early, like always. Chuck fetched her coat and saw her out, and it was outside there the deal was done. Like he was out there around twenty minutes and came in with lipstick all over his face, and grinning like an idiot. He headed straight for the bar and downed a scotch.'

'He announced the engagement?'

'Not in words he didn't, but nobody there was in any doubt. He'd let on he was going to ask her, and they'd been acting like an engaged couple all night.' Forrest gave a

135

sudden guilty look towards the french windows. 'Rita,' he said. 'Don't mention this to Rita! She's jealous enough as it is, and she'd blow her top if she knew the whole story.'

Gently nodded. 'And he'd have been outside twenty minutes, a little while after Pederson had left the mess.'

'Yeah, I guess.'

'And Pederson remained absent from the mess until the band had begun to pack up.'

'I have to admit that, fella, but it couldn't have been so long either. Chuck was back in while the last dance was going, and Kit slammed in straight after it finished.'

'So, all in all, he was out for most of an hour?'

Forrest scowled at him. 'If you say so.'

Gently finished his drink. 'Just getting the timing straight,' he said.

Forrest scowled some more, and also finished his drink. He slung the remains of his cigar in the bushes behind them. In the lounge they could see the four women watching them, one with a coffee-cup in her hand. Forrest gestured to the bottles.

'Pour you another?'

'Sorry, I'm driving,' Gently said.

Forrest frowned at the bottles for a moment, then shrugged. He turned to Gently.

'Listen fella,' he said. 'You've been straight with me and I've been straight with you. Which brings us back to where we came in. Are you going to hang this on Kit, or aren't you?'

'I can't answer that.' Gently met his gaze. 'As it stands, Pederson is a likely customer. But the evidence is indecisive, and as yet there is no case for the public prosecutor.'

'No case—as yet.'

Gently nodded.

'But something could still turn up, you think?'

'That is always possible.'

'But straight down the line! Do you reckon you'll hang it on Kit, or don't you?'

Gently let his eyes stray to the fields. 'If you're asking my opinion, I think it unlikely. The distance in time is too great. Suspicion may remain, but no element of proof.'

'Just suspicion.'

Gently nodded. 'Only one man now can ever know the truth.'

'You mean . . . Kit?'

'Kit. Or another.'

'Yeah,' Forrest said. 'Yeah.'

He let his eyes stray too. Across the fields the tractor had come into sight, a black midget seeming scarcely to move, with a flock of birds trailing behind it. Fields . . . Suffolk fields. Where once two Land Girls had laboured . . .

'I guess that's it then, Gently.' Forrest hoisted himself to his feet. 'I'll just say thank you for having this talk, and let you and your lady go on your way.' He held out his hand. 'You've eased my mind, fella, about this lousy business. Too bad it had to bug our trip, but that's how it goes. Guess we'll just have to live with it.'

Gently rose and took his hand. In the lounge, the ladies had risen too. Briefly, Forrest hung on to Gently.

'Perhaps—some other time,' he said.

*   *   *

'My dear, it was too ridiculous! Each one of those women could be a grandmother. Yet still they dye their hair and dress as though they were twenty. It is because they are Americans, ha? They wish people to think they are Hollywood stars?'

Gently shrugged as he drove. The ladies had come out to see them off—the hefty Mrs Forrest, the nervous Mrs Mitchell and the lean, stylish Rita Osborne, whose eyes had dwelt on him suspiciously. Unquestionably, their clothes were youthful, and their make-up had not been spared . . .

'And what do we talk about, yes? There is just one thing, and one thing only! It is about that poor Chuck Osborne, and how he is led astray by an English girl. Me, I am sorry for that man, he does not deserve such a wife as his Rita. After so long, still she is jealous, will blame him for ever for that young man's affair. Is it not laughable?'

Gently said: 'You wouldn't happen to have

mentioned how far it had gone?'

'My dear, it would scarcely have mattered, since the lady seemed to have no doubt. Those wicked English girls had only one thing in mind, to catch any Yank they could lay their hands on, and this one had laid her hands on Chuck. For sure, he meant to make her a GI bride.'

'You didn't offer confirmation.'

'Is your wife a fool? All the time I am pretending that I know nothing. And I am hearing the whole story of how naughty Chuck was letting her down. He is the boy-next-door, yes, and always they are intended for each other—from school, from growing-up, it is understood by them and by everyone. But then comes the war and poor Chuck is called up and sent overseas to this immoral country, and though, at first, she gets letters from him, as time is going on they become less frequent. She is alarmed, she talks to his mother, and oh dear!—his mother has a solemn face. In letters to her he mentions an English girl, and perhaps Rita should prepare herself for unwelcome news. She is crazy, she writes crazy letters, but no letters is she getting back. And for months this is going on and only the mother is getting news. Has she lost him—really lost him? At last, the news from the mother is good! This girl, this frightful Millicent, has vanished away, and cannot be found. Has she gone for ever? Yes, it appears so. From Chuck come numerous woeful letters, and finally even one for herself, in which the lying devil complains that he has had no letters from her! She pretends to believe him, yes? It is wartime, the post can go astray. And so, they come together again, and when he returns the wedding takes place. But forget it she cannot, no, never! Till the end of her days, she will not forget Millicent.' Gabrielle paused. 'Is it not too absurd?'

Gently merely shook his head.

'A brooch she was showing us,' Gabrielle said. 'A cheap brooch, but this he gives her on the day before he leaves for England. It is a token, yes? And she gives him one, a cigarette case on which are his initials. The brooch she still treasures, but the cigarette case, where is that?'

'Osborne lost it?'

'Aha, so he says! His dearest Rita has other ideas.'

'That he gave it to Miss Read?'

'What else? And this she will not be argued out of. Her friends tell her that this was wartime, that he was being moved from pillar to post, that their husbands were losing things too, but no good. He gave it to Millicent.' Gabrielle made a face of disgust. 'Do you know what I think, my friend?' she said. 'I think this business that happened here may be spelling the end of one marriage.'

'Have they any children?'

140

'A boy and a girl. But they are grown up and have children of their own.'

Gently slowed the car and let it idle. He hadn't taken a direct route back to Welbourne. Now they were passing on their left a ragged outcrop of concrete, and on their right, backed by trees . . .

Gabrielle grew suddenly alert.

'My dear—is this the place?'

Gently nodded.

'Then, please, let us stop! I wish to see it for myself.'

He halted the car. Gabrielle stared, at the cracked concrete, the forlorn hut. Peacefully it lay in the soft sunlight, remote, isolated, almost forgotten. No sign of a police presence had been left there, all the evidence that counted had been removed. Another dove was cooing in an oak tree. Beneath, sun fell on the bluebells.

'And it was really . . . here?' She sounded disappointed.

'In those days the mess-hall stood just over there. And then the domestic quarters, somewhere behind it. The airfield itself would have been across here.'

She shook her head. 'I cannot imagine! All this must have happened in another world. Now it is just these trees and bushes, and this old hut that seems not to belong.'

'Where you see that concrete was the door of the mess.'

She gazed. 'It was there he proposed to his Milly?'

'So he tells us.'

She paused. 'You do not believe him?'

'As you say, these things happened in another world.'

Gabrielle sighed. 'You know—I think! Perhaps it is best that they never found her. It is all too late. It belongs only to memories. She should have been left to sleep where they laid her. Is it not so?'

Gently merely gestured.

'Yes—and then all this trouble is avoided! Poor Chuck and his Rita are not quarrelling, and no one is heaping blame on his friend.'

'Unfortunately the discovery was made.'

'Then, it is best everyone forgets it. A tale from the war, no more. A mystery from when the Yanks were over here.'

Gently shrugged. The dove flew down, began pecking about on the concrete. There were other birds, tits, in the trees, and a rabbit peered for a moment from under the bushes. Another world!

He let in the clutch, drifted the Rover back towards Welbourne.

CHAPTER EIGHT

Had they got any further . . . and would they ever?

It was a certainty now that Pederson was lying. Whether he had left the toilets or not, he had been absent from the mess for longer than he was representing. Not the fifteen or twenty minutes it would have taken him to smoke a cheroot but a full hour, or near it, and leaving and returning in high dudgeon. Was it credible he had spent that time in the toilets, knowing what was going on, and feeling as he did?

Whether he would swear to it or not, there was little doubt what Bacon had seen that night. At some time Pederson had emerged from the toilets and made his way round the back of the mess. He knew within a little when Miss Read would be leaving, and would have timed his move accordingly . . . had it been his intention to catch Osborne afterwards, and to wreak vengeance on him out there?

Whatever, a loiterer in the shadows, he would have witnessed the scene that was enacting, the joyful acceptance of Miss Read, the epic of hugging and kissing that followed . . . had something snapped?

And then he had seen her, with customary firmness, send her happy swain back inside, and make her determined way through the black-out to collect her bicycle from the hut. He had lost her. His last hope was over. She was leaving, and leaving him. But . . . a final appeal, was that impossible, one more appeal to her generous nature? So he'd hastened after her, followed her into the hut, begged her, prayed her to think again, perhaps gone on his knees to heavenly Milly, but all, all to no avail. And suddenly she was falling, falling: falling from the hands that had gripped her too tight . . .

And after that?

He'd gone back to the mess. He was in a daze, but he wasn't stupid. Mechanically he'd gone through the motions, glared at Osborne, stood watching the band. Then, when the opportunity presented, he'd left with some others to return to the quarters, to wait there, sitting in his room, till everything had quietened down. Had the concrete where he buried her already been broken? The odds were that such had been the case. And, waiting there opportunely, had been a stack of oil-drenched engine-covers. So the job was done, the concrete replaced, and probably the remaining covers arranged over it. And her bike and handbag—they had to go: the pond through the trees was ready waiting for them.

A job well done! But . . . but . . .

Murderer Pederson went back to bed. Could it really have happened, wasn't it simply a dream, a nightmare triggered by that night in the mess?

Mechanically still he'd risen with the others, fastened his chute, got into his plane, flown, flown, still locked in his dream, till suddenly he was plunging earthwards . . .

However obscured by half a century, that was the picture standing out, the picture asserted by Miss Read's workmate and only reluctantly denied by Major Forrest. Evidence and proof there was not, merely the pointer of circumstance, while any alternative theories were too vague to admit consideration. Time had won. Eyke might ferret on, but the chance of bringing a case to court was remote . . .

'Stop at the shop if you will, my dear.'

Gabrielle could rarely bear to pass it. Gently parked at the nearest slot and took the opportunity to light his pipe. Then, as he puffed, there came a tap at his window. It was Sid, the landlord of The Bell, with a shopping bag in his hand.

'Your missus told me I'd find you here . . . I thought I ought to have a word! That Yank who was in the pub yesterday—you remember him? Well, now he's asking if I've got a room.'

'You mean Osborne?'

'He didn't tell me his name. That tall old bloke with a lot of grey hair.'

Gently nodded.

'I don't know,' Sid said. 'But I've had him around all day. I wouldn't say he was boozed, but he's had plenty, and we gave him some sandwiches for his lunch. He just sits there staring at nobody, and a while ago he was asking about a room. Do you think he's all right?'

'Is he there now?'

'Sitting in the garden when I left,' Sid said. 'I'd just given him a refill. But I don't know, I don't feel too happy about him having a room. What do you say?'

Gently blew a smoke-ring. 'I don't think he's dangerous!' he said. 'Just a man with a problem.'

'I daresay. But with this rum business going on at Toddington and all.'

'I'll talk to him,' Gently said. 'You say he's in the garden?'

'On a bench out there.'

'Have a pint ready.'

Sid departed on his way and shortly Gabrielle reappeared, a bundle of magazines in her hand. Gently briefly explained, and advised her to take the car back to Heatherings. Gabrielle looked grave.

'So, it is beginning,' she said. 'That terrible Rita! Are you sure I should not come with you?'

'Better not,' Gently said. 'By now he may be a little drunk.'

'I feel so sorry for that man.'

Gently shrugged and climbed out of the car.

Five minutes later, pint in hand, he was sitting down opposite the forlorn Osborne.

146

'Fella, I can do without you!'

Osborne's glass was nearly empty again. Clearly he had put down quite a few of them during his long stint at The Bell. His square-cut features were rosy and his bushy hair dishevelled, and he sat slumped with his elbows resting on the table of the bench. But the hazel eyes that met Gently's had every appearance of alertness. He stared at him sullenly, his mouth in a pout.

Gently took a pull from his glass. 'I've just come from Toddington,' he said.

'Yeah? So what?'

'The Major requested that we should have a talk.'

Osborne's eyes flickered. 'You see my wife?'

'We were introduced,' Gently said. 'My own wife accompanied me. She was left to talk with the ladies while the Major and I had our chat.'

'She talked to my wife?'

'To all the ladies. They had coffee together in the lounge.'

'You think . . . she told her?'

Gently shook his head.

Osborne stared into his glass. 'Guess she didn't need to.'

Gently knocked out his pipe in a tray already full of cigarette stubs, slowly refilled and lit it. Osborne watched him with steady eyes.

'You talk about me to the Major?' he said.

Gently puffed smoke over his head. 'We talked about everything,' he said. 'About all that happened that night of the dance.'

'Like—me and her?'

'About that. The Major was there and saw it going on. He was able to fill in some gaps in the information we have.'

His stare was rigid. 'And Rita—she could hear this?'

'Your wife was in the lounge with the others.'

'But where were you, for chrissake!'

'We were sitting at a table out on the lawn.'

'She couldn't hear?'

'No. Our conversation was entirely private.'

Osborne scooped up the glass and tossed back the contents, set the glass down with a shaky hand. On the table was a pack of Chesterfields. He pulled one out and lit it. He sucked smoke.

'So what did Robbie tell you?'

'He described the proceedings.'

'Like how I was whooping it up with Milly?'

'He gave me an account of that.'

'Yeah, I bet.' Osborne hissed smoke. 'How we were dancing cheek to cheek. Like you could read it all over us. Like Hitler himself couldn't have broken us up. Ain't that how it went?'

Gently shrugged.

'So I loved that girl,' Osborne said. 'Let everyone know. Let the world hear it. Put it on a tape and play it to Rita.' He coughed. 'I never could get over it. When she went missing I nearly died. I just couldn't believe she would leave me cold, right after that night she gave me her word. It was too crazy. All I could think was that some other guy had kidnapped her.'

'You had no suspicions at the time?'

'Yeah, this stupid idea I'm telling you.'

'That she was kidnapped?'

He nodded. 'At first I was thinking it was one of our lot. But I couldn't figure it, how it was worked. And then I got another idea. You got to remember we weren't too popular with a lot of people over here.'

Gently paused. 'You mean the farm people?'

'Hell no—though they may have had a hand in it! No, I mean her family back home, who she used to tell me about. They were nice people and she was fond of them, especially a kid brother in the RAF. But I got the idea from her that Yanks were not their favourite people, and maybe they got a tip-off that she was going to sign up with one of them.'

'And they—kidnapped her?'

'Yeah.' He puffed. 'I know it sounds a bit crazy now, fella! But not then it didn't. She'd disappeared, and your police couldn't find the smallest trace. So like someone could have been waiting for her when she got back to the

149

farm that night, and she was just bundled into a car and driven off back to the Derbyshire place.'

'And kept there against her will?'

'Yeah, I guess. Maybe they'd got it fixed up.'

'And the farm people knew about this?'

'Maybe yes. And maybe no. The father showed up and talked to the police, but that could have been an act he put on.'

Gently drank. 'And had you any suspicion of who it was that may have tipped the family off?'

'Yeah.' He nodded. 'My guess was that little pal of hers who worked with her at the farm. We saw her around with Milly in the pub and she surely had it in for us Yanks. Kit tried to persuade her to come to the dances, but she just stuck her chin out at him.'

'He tried to chat her up?'

'I guess. But Milly was the one we were really after.'

He lit another Chesterfield from the first, and stubbed the latter in the tray. His fingers were trembling. He kept his eyes on the empty glass in front of him. Gently said:

'But now we know. It wasn't a question of Miss Read being kidnapped.'

'Please, fella.'

'Also, we know a little more of what went on that evening.'

'Fella, I don't want to hear!'

'Tell me one thing,' Gently said. 'After what

went on between you outside the mess, why didn't you insist on accompanying Miss Read when she went to fetch her bike?'

'I told you, she wouldn't let me.'

'But what was her reason?'

'Oh, for chrissake—because she was Milly!'

'And you didn't insist? You let the girl you were just engaged to depart through the black-out to an unlit hut?'

'Yeah—yeah.' He squirmed on the bench. 'You didn't know her, how she was. Milly was tough, that's why I loved her. When she made her mind up, you went along.'

'But she gave no reason.'

'Sure she gave a reason! Like she was late and didn't want me to hold her up.'

'And—you accepted that?'

'Fella, what are you getting at?'

Gently took a long pull from his glass. He said: 'In accepting you that evening Miss Read had to turn another suitor down. It was in her nature to do it as gently as possible, and twice that evening she had danced with him, trying to console him. But he wasn't consoled, and she was aware of it. May she not have been expecting a final encounter with him?'

'With—Kit?'

Gently nodded.

'But that sod had cleared off to the toilets!'

'Some understanding she may have had with him.'

Osborne glared, then shook his head with

151

vigour.

'Isn't it a possibility?'

'No, it sodding isn't!' He stared hard into Gently's eyes. 'You're after him, aren't you? You'd cook up anything, even crazy ideas like this.'

'Is it so crazy?'

'Yes, it is! Milly wouldn't have pulled a trick like that. And Kit knew it was over, that he didn't have a chance. That's why he took off and went to sulk in the toilets.'

'For . . . nearly an hour?'

'He wasn't gone that long.'

'That time has been supplied by Major Forrest.' Gently blew one of his rings. 'And, in addition, we have testimony from another witness. Pederson was seen to emerge from the toilets at about the time that you and Miss Read were outside the mess.'

His eyes were large. 'You're stringing me along, fella!'

Gently blew another ring. And shook his head.

*   *   *

There were dregs left in Osborne's glass and he tossed them back and slammed the glass down heavily. The cigarette was trembling between his fingers, and a moment later it was stubbed among its predecessors. He gave Gently a flickering look.

'So this guy . . . who was he?'

Gently shrugged. 'A civilian doing a job in the women's toilets. He had occasion to fetch a tool from outside, and while out there saw a serviceman leave the other toilets.'

'A civilian! Then he couldn't swear . . .'

'He was familiar with the camp and the personnel.'

'But it needn't have been Kit!'

'According to Pederson, he was alone in the toilets at that time.'

'He could have come out for a breath of air . . .'

Gently shook his head. 'He was seen to depart round the end of the mess. It involved him passing in front of a semi-lit window which enabled the witness to get a sight of him.'

'So the bastard is lying!'

'I think not.'

'Then it wasn't that evening!'

Gently was silent.

Osborne snatched his stare away and gazed scowlingly at the door to the bar. Some of the rosiness had left his cheeks and he couldn't control the shake in his hands. Suddenly, he was looking his age: a man several decades past his prime.

Gently said: 'How long were you out there in the company of Miss Read?'

'Fella . . . lay off me.'

'Was it a few minutes or was it, perhaps, nearer half an hour?'

153

'Fella, lay off!' His mouth was quivering.

'You can surely recall an occasion so important.'

'Like I wasn't watching a clock—I'd got other things on my mind!'

'So?'

'For bloody chrissake, I was there as long as it took! And that's to say as long as she let me—it wasn't me who broke it up.'

'You were guided by her.'

'Yeah. Yeah.'

'She left you standing there.'

'Yeah.'

'You watched her depart in the direction of the hut.'

He made a desperate gesture with his shaking hands. 'She wouldn't have it—she shoved me towards the door. She said we'd have plenty of time later, and I was to go in, and not miss the last dance.'

'And you went in?'

'I'm telling you, fella!'

Slowly Gently shook his head. 'I think you would have hung on,' he said. 'Just a moment. Just till her footsteps died away.'

'And—I'm saying I didn't!'

He shook out a fresh Chesterfield, but was barely able to get his lighter to function.

Gently struck a fresh light for his pipe and took his time in applying it. He puffed a few times. He said:

'At no time were you conscious of being

154

overlooked?'

'No I wasn't!'

'That couldn't have been the reason that Miss Read so abruptly broke up the party?'

'Oh, for crying out, fella!'

'Think about it,' Gently puffed. 'Twice that evening Miss Read had tried to console your friend, and she had seen him strut out of the mess in a disturbed state of mind. Then later, outside, she becomes aware of a watcher, and at once she thinks of Pederson. So she hurries you in—if there is to be a third encounter she doesn't want it to be in front of you. Does that sound unreasonable?'

'Hell no!'

'Pederson was certainly out there, Osborne.'

'It was the black-out, she couldn't have seen . . .'

'She could have heard movement.'

'She—no!'

Gently puffed. 'I think it likely,' he said. 'And if she could hear him, so could you. And if you wanted to you could tell me.'

Osborne writhed. He was shaking helplessly, trying to get the cigarette to his lips. At last he managed a puff or two, then let the cigarette fall on the ashtray.

'Well?'

'You . . . lousy bastard!'

'You did hear someone about there.'

'Suppose I did? I couldn't see him, and you're never going to make me say it was

Kit . . .'

'But—someone you heard?'

'Yeah . . . I thought. And maybe Milly heard it too. And yeah, it was then she broke it up and started shoving me towards the door.'

'Could you place the sound?'

He nodded. 'Some place down the far end of the mess, like someone had stepped on a twig. Too far for the guy to have heard what we were saying.'

'But . . . Miss Read responded by sending you back in.'

'Yeah.' His lips quivered. 'You could put it like that.'

'And you—you had no thought of who the watcher might have been?'

He grabbed the cigarette back and took several quick puffs.

'Well?'

'Not then I didn't. Not till I got back in the mess. Then I thought . . . like you. And sure, it worried me for a bit! But I knew Kit was on a loser, and I could see it in his face when he came in.'

'Did you speak to him about it?'

'Why would I? The guy was avoiding me like the plague.'

'Not the next morning?'

'Nope. And you know what happened after that.'

'But . . . since?'

He mauled the cigarette. 'Listen, fella, I

don't know nothing! Who that guy was back there, or whether it was him who did that to Milly. I don't know and I'm not saying. All that happened too far back. You guys can think what you like about it, but nothing you get out of Chuck Osborne.'

'You won't give us a statement.'

'Nope.'

'It may leave us thinking there is something to hide.'

'Then I guess you'll just have to think it.'

And tremulously, he turned his back on Gently.

*   *   *

Did he really know more than he was admitting?

Gently frowned at the slumped figure sitting across from him. There must have been talk back there at the Old Rectory, exchanges between himself and Pederson. Pederson didn't know that he had been spotted leaving the toilets and neither, till now, did Osborne, but the latter had been aware of a watcher and was in little doubt about who it must have been. Deadly rivals they may have been then, but today, five decades later . . . He shook his head! Two old comrades in arms, the likelihood was they had reached an understanding, a pact to stand each by the other. And guided perhaps by the sage Major

157

Forrest . . .

Sid appeared at the door to the bar and made a gesture towards the glasses, but Gently waved him away. Wasn't it worth just one more pass? He knocked out his pipe. He said:

'Isn't it a fact that Miss Read was reluctant to come to a decision, and that you had been pressing her for quite some time before, on your testimony, she conceded?'

For a moment it didn't sink in. Then he jerked about, his eyes wide.

'Just what are you getting at, fella?'

Gently shrugged. 'Isn't that the situation?'

'You're telling me I'm a liar?'

'I'm saying that it rests on your word. What happened between you outside the mess.'

'But it's the truth—everyone knew!'

Gently shook his head.

'Yes—Kit can tell you!'

'All Kit can tell me is that she had intentions. But she may have changed them when she got outside.'

'But that's crazy! Why would she?'

'Because, all along, she would appear to have had doubts. She had ambitions for a career when the war was over, ambitions that marrying an American would have overturned.'

'You're crazy, fella—crazy!'

'It fits with her character as we know it. For a while, that evening, she was carried away, but when it came to the point, her better

158

judgement took over. So she sought to dismiss you into the mess while she went alone to collect her bicycle.'

'But it wasn't like that!'

'On your word alone.'

'Fella, I can't believe what I'm hearing!'

'It fits the facts as we know them.'

'It can't—never!'

Gently shrugged and took a sip from his glass.

Osborne was trembling, gazing at nothing, a desperate look in his eyes. One of his hands was grasping the lighter, the other the edge of the table. After a pause, Gently said:

'Wouldn't it be possible that you went along with her—still unable to accept your dismissal, and hopeful of urging her to change her mind?'

'No—I can't believe this, fella!'

'It would have been the natural thing to have done. She had come so close to giving you her word, and a little extra persuasion may have been successful.'

He slammed the lighter on the table. 'Are you saying it was me who killed her?'

'I'm looking at the facts I have in front of me.'

'The facts—they're not the sodding facts!'

Gently nodded. 'You deny them?'

'Yeah—a couple of million times!' He ground his teeth, stared Gently in the face. 'You ain't going to believe me, are you? But those are the facts that I told you, the facts they wrote down and had me sign.'

Gently said: 'The facts . . . but short of one detail.'

'Short of nothing, hear me telling you!'

'Short of a mention that another person was outside there along with yourself and Miss Read.'

'You . . . lousy cop!' His breathing came fast. 'You want me to give him away, don't you?'

Gently shrugged.

'Yeah—and that's what this is all about! You know Milly gave me her word and it went the way I told you—Kit's the poor guy you're after and me, I'm to knock in the last nail.'

Gently gave him a cool stare.

'So nothing,' he said. 'Sodding nothing! I didn't see anyone, didn't hear anyone, all it was was Milly and me.'

'We have an independent witness, Mr Osborne.'

'So stick to your lousy independent witness!'

'You have admitted being aware of a third person's presence.'

'So that's your tale, but it ain't going to be mine.'

Gently said: 'You could just do yourself a favour by including that point in your testimony.'

Osborne glared at him. 'Forget it,' he said. 'You've made your play, but it isn't going to win.'

160

He turned his back on Gently again and fumbled for another Chesterfield. Perhaps he was trembling just a little less now, as though he may have felt he had scored a point. Perhaps he had? He struck a light first time, and tilted the cigarette at an angle. Gently drank up. And then, at that moment, a woman's voice could be heard in the bar. Osborne froze.

'Goddamn it—Rita!'

He hauled himself up, looked round for some avenue of escape. But it was too late. Escorted by Sid, Rita Osborne came striding out into the garden. Her flashing eyes fixed on Osborne.

'Chuck! So this is where you've been hiding out.'

'Rita—please!'

'Yes, and by the look of you you haven't been wasting your time here. What little game are you playing, Chuck?'

'Rita . . . honestly!'

'Oh, I think I can guess. But the game is over now, my son. And the car is waiting for you outside.'

'Rita listen! We've got to talk . . .'

'We surely have. So get in that car.'

Helplessly he stared at her, then snatched up his cigarettes and lighter. A gate gave access to the road from the garden and, unsteadily, he made his way towards it. Sid faded diplomatically back into the bar. Rita

Osborne flashed a look at Gently.

'Don't bother to tell me,' she said. 'I can guess what's been going on. You found him here half-cut and you haven't been wasting your time, either. So what did it buy you fella—was it Chuck who did for that little tart?'

Gently made her a smile, and shook his head.

'Don't think it bothers me,' Rita Osborne said. 'The way I'm feeling about Chuck this moment you can lock him up and welcome. He was going to marry that tart, I know it and so do you. If he changed his mind and strangled her instead that's no skin off my nose.' Her stare was keen. 'You got it out of him?' she said. 'He was going to marry the bitch?'

Gently picked up his pipe, blew through it and slipped it in his pocket.

'So I don't get told,' Rita Osborne said. 'And your froggy wife wasn't letting on either. But don't think you're kidding me. I can smell a rat. And I've known rotten Chuck for a few years now.'

'Half a century ago,' Gently said. 'Half a century.'

'Whaddya mean, half a century ago?'

'Fifty-three years and some months.'

She stared at him angrily. 'And that's all I get told?'

'It may be worth remembering,' Gently said. 'The better part of a lifetime.'

She stared harder. Then gave her head a toss. 'You men,' she said. 'You lousy men.'

Gently turned to hide his expression.

'Why the hell do we bother?' Rita Osborne said. 'It's a mystery to me.'

And she strode after her husband.

CHAPTER NINE

'This confounded business at Toddington, Gently—I want you to lay it on the line! That fellow—what's his name?—Major Forrest has been on to his embassy, and they've been on to me.'

Gently had seen the blue Mercedes in the drive and knew pretty well what to expect. Sitting in the lounge, with a glass at his elbow, was the local Chief Constable, Sir Thomas Bedingfield. They were old acquaintances. Gently had barely moved in there when Sir Tommy had first grabbed him for an assignment, and ever since, when the occasion arose, he had applied for the Yard man's services.

Not an association entirely without friction—Gently's methods had sometimes roused Sir Tommy's indignation! But, when the chips were down, he had never hesitated to fetch him in.

Today he was looking a little fierce, but that

was too usual to occasion comment.

'The point is this. Those blasted Yanks more or less told me to turn it in. What we're dealing with here is a set of war heroes, and heaven help us if we drag them into it. They seem to have got the impression from Forrest that we're damn-near making an arrest, and if we want to hang on to the special relationship we've got to drop it right there.' Sir Tommy snorted. 'I kept my temper, but I came close to telling them off. Hell and all, if there's a case there, do they really expect us to cover it up?' He leered at Gently. 'I've talked to Eykey,' he said. 'Eykey thinks there just could be one. That Pederson chappie. From what Eykey tells me there isn't much doubt that he's our chummie. But you're the man with your finger in it—as usual, and now I want to hear from you. In so many words, George Gently, are you expecting to bring a charge?'

Gently shrugged, and sat down.

'Yes or no?' Sir Tommy demanded.

'As of now?'

'As of now.'

Slowly Gently shook his head.

Sir Tommy's stare grew fiercer. 'Let me get this right,' he said. 'There's a case there, you're telling me, but as yet we haven't quite got it made.'

Gently nodded.

'But you bloody expect to?'

'Some . . . fresh detail . . . could arise.'

164

'That's all it needs?'

After a pause, Gently nodded again.

Sir Tommy snorted. 'Get this clear,' he said. 'I'm in a tricky situation. If any case does come out of this it has to be one that's cut and dried. I can't afford a lame-duck prosecution with these people on my back, any charge has got to stick. Less than that, and it doesn't go forward. Are you with me?'

Another nod.

'A signed confession is what we need here. A confession supported by independent testimony that will stand up to cross-examination. Give me that, and we go to court, but anything less and we forget it.' He made a noise between a snort and a sigh. 'Perhaps it would be better to do that anyway!'

Gently shrugged. 'It's an unusual case.'

Sir Tommy jerked his head. 'So they've been telling me! Fifty years ago, and there was a war on, how can we expect to get to the bottom of it? A mystery of the war, that's what they're calling it. So bury the bones and let sleeping dogs lie—they've even offered to send a wreath if I send them details of the funeral.'

Gently said: 'Her brother is still alive and is hoping to inter the remains at their home town in Derbyshire.'

'Her brother.' Sir Tommy frowned. 'It's hard to think of that skeleton as a person. Do we know much about her?'

'A little,' Gently said. 'She is said to have

165

been a cultivated girl, and to have taken her duties at the farm conscientiously.'

'A bit of a looker?'

'A blonde.'

'Liked the fellows?'

'She wasn't averse to them. But apparently she wasn't a push-over. After the war, she intended to be a teacher.'

'Damn,' Sir Tommy said. 'Damn.' He turned his stare on the garden outside. 'A bit like my own sister,' he said. 'She was a teacher. But she wasn't a blonde. It brings it home to you, doesn't it?'

'A girl at the outset of her life. Who moments earlier had plighted her troth.'

'You don't have to rub it in!' Sir Tommy felt for his glass. 'Fifty years or yesterday,' he said after a sip. 'The bastard who did that ought to pay for it.'

Gently shrugged.

'Just how close are you?'

'Fairly close,' Gently admitted. 'But the evidence is all circumstantial, and I don't expect to obtain a confession.'

'But there's a chance—a chance of a breakthrough?'

'In one direction it is possible.'

'Enough to fix him. To fix Pederson?'

'It may not be enough to take to court.'

'Not enough.' Sir Tommy shook his head. 'Well, now you know the situation, George. If you can nail him I'll be cheering, but it's all or nothing with friend Pederson. Understood?'

'Understood.'

'Then I'll leave it in your capable hands. And just ask you to remember that when it comes to the push, we'll be up against the best counsel that dollars can buy.' He grounded his unfinished glass and rose. 'There's no need to see me out.'

Moments later came the sound of the Mercedes being reversed, and the scatter of gravel as Sir Tommy drove away.

*   *   *

For a while, Gently sat watching the ranks of daffodils beside the lawn. So that was the situation . . . but hadn't he known it all along? Slowly the case had built up against Pederson, a detail here, a detail there: a little more, and in the normal way they would have to be considering an arrest. But . . . this wasn't the normal way! Here, they were dealing with a distant past, a world existing in hazy memory, a world uncheckable, beyond possible clues. And the man they were pursuing, as Sir Tommy had pointed out, was a man with powerful influence behind him. A mystery of the war . . . was there anything to gain by pressing the matter yet further?

Some certainty they might arrive at and the guilt lay firmly at its proper door, but no more. And what end would it serve, if the truth of the affair could never be published? So long it had weighed on the conscience of the culprit, a far-off horror, a haunting dream: so let it stay: let his days end without the final arraignment branded upon him. Eyke, without doubt, had received his warning, and no blame would attach if Gently dropped the matter there . . .

'My dear, I heard all that!'

He turned, to find Gabrielle beside him.

'Sir Tommy arrived here in quite a tiz, and I thought it best to sit him down with a glass of whisky. To me, he has nothing to say, except to ask if you would be long, so I leave him with his whisky—but take care not to be far away!' She paused. 'And so it shall be, hah? You will let the dogs sleep, as the Americans say?'

Gently found a wry grin. 'It may end that way. We don't have the sort of case that Sir Tommy insists on.'

'This man Pederson—you will let him go home?'

'As yet we have nothing that will keep him here.'

'And that is O.K. ?'

'It may be best.'

'You just let him go?'

Gently nodded.

Gabrielle considered the daffodils. 'I do not know, my friend,' she said. 'Once I am thinking like the Americans, but, when I hear you tell of that girl! She was a little special, yes? One who is doing her duty in the war, a good girl, one with ambitions, a girl who likes her fun but is not carried away. Such a girl I could have been friends with, and to her this terrible thing happens. This I cannot forget, nor can I accept that the Yank goes unpunished.'

Gently said: 'He has his conscience.'

'Hah. But what is that to such a man? Once, perhaps, he is regretting, but this will not last very long.'

'The following day he was shot down.'

'Is not enough for such a crime! Still he has his own life, yes, he comes back to live, to prosper, to be happy? No, no, my friend, he lives, while that poor girl is under the concrete. This man I cannot forgive, for such a crime he should answer.'

Gently toyed with his pipe. 'You could be right.'

'For him, it may even be a relief. If he has this conscience of which you speak it may help him lay it to rest.'

Gently shrugged.

'No.' She turned to him. 'You are still letting these dogs sleep?'

He shook his head. 'You heard Sir Tommy. Only a supported confession can go forward.'

'And this will not happen?'

'Almost certainly there will be no confession from Pederson. And if there were, the supporting testimony we have obtained will be insufficient. The sort of counsel they will retain for him will make short work of that.'

'So . . . he gets away with it?'

Gently sighed. 'At the moment I can see no other ending. We have come to the matter too late. So perhaps it is time to begin forgetting it.'

'To forget—that?'

'Yes.'

Gabrielle returned her attention to the daffodils. 'I am not forgetting it,' she said. 'That young girl. To die then, at such a moment. And this man, who lives his whole life afterwards. But from my mind I will try to put it. Will this do?'

'It will do.'

'Then it is time we had our tea and I will speak to Mrs Jarvis.'

But before she could leave the room another car could be heard crunching the gravel, to be followed by the sound of not one, but two doors, slamming. Gabrielle hesitated.

'Can it be Andy? We are not expecting him today?'

Gently shook his head. Shortly, Mrs Jarvis came to the door.

'Two ladies for you, Mr Gently. Would you like me to show them in?'

'Two ladies?'

'One is a Mrs Bacon. The other one's name I didn't catch.'

Gabrielle's eye caught Gently's, then lifted to the ceiling.

'Show them in, please,' Gently said.

'Mrs Oakley, she's my neighbour. I'll tell you in a minute why I brought her along.'

Cissy Bacon had nearly collided with Gabrielle as the latter hastened to vacate the lounge. She had with her a tall, elderly lady, who smiled uneasily when she was introduced. Cissy Bacon appropriated a chair next to Gently and pointed to another for her friend.

'You sit there, Madge, don't stand on ceremony.'

The tall lady cautiously took the chair. Cissy Bacon glanced towards the door, perhaps to make certain it was shut, then leaned forward and fixed her dark eyes on Gently's.

'Now—Kit Pederson! Have you pulled him in yet?'

Gently's stare was expressionless.

'Oh, get along with you!' Cissy Bacon said. 'You know he did it as well as I do. And don't worry about Madge here because she's heard all about it.'

Mrs Oakley attempted a smile, but finished up gazing down at her folded hands.

'So—have you or haven't you? I'd like to know that before we go on. If you've already arrested him and made a charge you perhaps don't need to hear what I've come to tell you.'

Gently's blank stare continued. He said: 'You have come here with information?'

171

'Don't make me laugh! Why else would I be here? And you haven't answered the question.'

Was there a hint of anxiety in those thrusting eyes? She was tightly grasping the handbag on her lap. Her friend was still gazing down at her hands and seemed to be wishing she was somewhere else. Gently said:

'No arrest has been made and no arrest is contemplated.'

'You mean—you don't have enough on him yet?'

'I mean exactly what I say.'

'Yes,' Cissy Bacon said. 'I get you. And perhaps there's something we can do about that.' She leaned back. 'Bert,' she said. 'He's the stumbling block, isn't he? If you could get Bert to speak up you could put your hand on Pederson's shoulder.'

Gently stared but said nothing.

Cissy Bacon nodded. 'And that's why we've come here. You were never going to get it out of him on your own so I thought it was time I lent you a hand.' She glanced across at her friend. 'Madge,' she said. 'We set it up this afternoon.'

'You set it up?'

'We certainly did.'

'Oh Cissy!' Mrs Oakley said.

'Well, I had to do something,' Cissy Bacon said. 'It was up to me, Madge. And Milly was my mate.'

Mrs Oakley shook her head but was silent.

'So,' Gently said. 'What was it you set up?'

'I'll tell you. Bert was in the garden, it's about all he ever does these days, so I kept an eye on him, and waited till he was safely tucked away in the greenhouse. Then I gave Madge the signal, and she slipped round to ours, and I sat her down by the service-hatch in the dining-room. I'd got the kettle boiling of course, and I made two mugs of tea, and went to call Bert. So there he was in the kitchen drinking his tea, him on one side of the hatch, Madge on the other. And maybe you can guess the rest.'

'Oh it was awful!' Mrs Oakley said. 'Poor Bert hadn't the remotest idea I was there.'

'No, it was just him and me—having a little talk about you know what.'

'You led him on!' Mrs Oakley said.

'I had to, Madge. It was the only way.'

'Yes, but if he'd known . . .'

'Well he didn't. And now you can tell the Superintendent what you heard.'

Mrs Oakley twisted her hands. 'I suppose I shall have to,' she said. 'But I feel mean, Cissy. It's like telling tales about an old friend.' Nervously she turned towards Gently. 'Cissy was asking him about that night,' she said. 'The night when it happened, when he was working late in one of the toilets. It wasn't fair, really! She said now they were alone he needn't be so cagey. And she asked him if it was really Pederson he saw leaving the toilets,

173

and if he could swear to it if he ever had to. And he said yes, because when he first saw him he'd been lighting a cheroot, so he could see who it was.'

Gently said: 'Those were his words—that he could see the man was Pederson?'

'Yes, but he said he was never going to admit it, because it all happened so long ago.'

Gently nodded. 'Carry on!'

Mrs Oakley stared at her hands. 'Cissy asked him if he saw where the man went, and he said yes, towards the hut.'

'He mentioned the hut?'

'Yes.'

'Specifically the hut—not just in that direction?'

'Cissy—she asked him if the man went into it, but he said he couldn't see that because of the black-out. She kept on at him about it but he wouldn't say any more than that. Then she asked him if he'd heard anything suspicious going on there, but he said no, it was too far away.'

'Was there anything else?'

'No . . . I don't think so. He began to get fed up with Cissy going on at him. He said he wanted to forget all about it and he wished the Americans had never come there. Then I heard him put down his mug and go out through the door.'

'So,' Cissy Bacon said. 'Now you know. The man Bert saw going off there was Pederson.

174

You've got my word and Madge's for that, and Bert is going to have to admit it. What more do you need?'

Gently regarded her. 'I think a word with your husband,' he said.

'You think we're telling you a tale?'

He shook his head. 'Just corroboration from the man himself. Where will I find him?'

Her eyes were angry. 'In the garden. Where we left him. But Bert will keep. What you should be doing now is getting your hands on Pederson. If you leave it any longer you may find he's done a bunk.'

Staring at the window, Gently said: 'Your attitude to Pederson still surprises me. To have lasted for so long, it seems to call for an explanation.'

What else besides anger was in that stare? She snatched at her bag and jumped from the chair.

'And suppose I told you he'd raped me! Would that help you to understand?'

'Oh Cissy, please!' her friend pleaded.

'Did he rape you?' Gently said.

'He could have done. There was plenty going on in those days, you only had to go outside with one of them.'

'But—did he?'

'You'll never know, will you?'

Gently gazed at her. And shrugged.

'Oh, come on Madge!' Cissy Bacon said. 'It's up to him what happens now. We've told

175

him what we came here to tell him, and now we'll leave him to get on with it.'

'Wait,' Gently said.

'You've had your chips!'

'I was going to request a lift to your bungalow.'

'You—you've got a nerve,' she said. 'I've half a mind to tell you to go to hell.'

*　　　*　　　*

They dropped Mrs Oakley at the gate of the bungalow and drove in to park in the drive. Nothing had been said on that short trip by either of the two ladies. Now, wordlessly, Cissy Bacon slammed the car door, pointed to the garden, and strutted into the house, to be met by a black cat which had to jump aside alertly to avoid being trodden on.

Gently made his way past the garage to an extensive lawn and flowerbeds, then through a rustic fence to the kitchen garden beyond. There was a shed and a greenhouse. It was in the latter that he encountered Herbert Bacon. The retired builder was occupied in potting seedlings and, for a moment, chose to ignore his visitor. Then he wiped compost from his calloused fingers and slowly turned to face Gently.

'Cissy . . . she's been after you again?'

There was a quaver in his voice. He looked round for something to help with the wiping, but finished by polishing his hands on his trousers.

'You want to go inside?'

'We can talk here.'

'There isn't nothing else I can tell you.'

'Perhaps . . . if we go over what you told me again?'

'Can't see what good that's going to do you.'

In a corner of the greenhouse was an empty crate: Gently turned it on its end to make a seat. After a moment, Herbert Bacon pulled a stool from under the bench he'd been working on, and cautiously lowered himself on it.

Lean, frail-looking, with withered features, there was still deep intelligence in the watery grey eyes. He went on polishing his hands, waiting for Gently to make his move. Gently said:

'An hour or more ago, did your wife call you in for a mug of tea?'

Herbert Bacon seemed to think about it. 'Is that what she was after you with?'

'You remember the conversation you had with her?'

He bowed his head. 'She was on about the same old thing. But don't you pay too much attention to Cissy. She's got a bee in her bonnet about that fellow.'

'About Pederson.'

'Yes.'

'Who you saw leaving the toilets that night.'

'She'd like me to say so.'

'But you still are not certain?'

'I can't be, can I, after all that time.'

'Even though you got a look at his face?'

'If she told you that she was making it up.'

'When he lit that cheroot?'

'What cheroot? I never mentioned anything about cheroots to Cissy.'

Gently said: 'Soon after you went in for your tea, did you hear your wife drive off in her car?'

'Must have done,' Herbert Bacon said. 'She'd have been going after you, wouldn't she.'

'Did you see her leave?'

'I looked across there. I don't pay much attention to what she does. Seems she was giving our neighbour a lift. She must have gone on to yours afterwards.'

'Would that neighbour have been Mrs Oakley?'

'Madge Oakley. She lives in that house next-door.'

'A woman you know?'

'Can't help it, can I? She's all right, I get on with Madge.'

'A woman you wouldn't expect to tell lies.'

His watery gaze looked puzzled.

'I regret having to inform you,' Gently said. 'That she overheard that conversation with your wife. Your wife had installed Mrs Oakley in your dining-room for that precise purpose. She was seated close to the service-hatch which I assume would have been left open, and was able to recount to me what passed between you in the kitchen. Would you have noticed that the hatch was open?'

His stare at Gently was aghast. 'Cissy—did that?'

'I'm afraid she did.'

'But I can't believe—!'

Gently shrugged. 'So perhaps we can come to the point,' he said. 'You did recognise Pederson that night, and you saw him leave in the direction of the Nissen-hut.'

But Herbert Bacon didn't seem to be listening. He was gazing helplessly at the pots of seedlings, his hands still unconsciously massaging his trousers. Then he glanced at Gently. And quickly away.

'Well?'

'It's one of Cissy's tricks—it has to be! Madge and her are in it together.'

'Are you saying they cooked all this up?'

'Yes—that fellow. She could never stand him!'

'She has something against Pederson?'

He kept his eyes on the pots. 'Perhaps I shouldn't be telling you this. But yes, she's always had it in for him. It—it was something that happened in the old days!'

'Something . . . ?'

He nodded. 'They met in the pub. It was before Cissy and me got together. He bought her drinks, and she thought he fancied her, but that was before he got to know Milly. After that he wouldn't look at her, but she was determined she was going to have him. She wrote him a letter, like it was from Milly, asking him to meet her, I don't remember where.'

'And he did meet her?'

'Yes. And when she came back she had a black eye. She swore she'd do for him if she ever got a chance, and when she heard he was shot down she danced a little jig. I shouldn't have told you, but you've got to know. She'll stop at nothing to get him put away.'

'So . . . she invented that whole conversation?'

He nodded to the pots. 'Her and Madge.'

'Pederson was never mentioned.'

'No. It's all made up.'

Gently said softly: 'You're lying, aren't you?'

Herbert Bacon went on wiping his hands.

*   *   *

Down the garden, across the lawn, Cissy Bacon could be seen at one of the windows. It was too far off to distinguish her expression but her gaze never shifted from the direction of the greenhouse. Two seated figures was all she saw, obscured by the vines of tomato plants, but the gaze never wavered. She could perhaps barely see the face of her husband turned away from that of his interrogator.

180

Below the window, on a tiled patio, the black cat was lying stretched out in a patch of sun.

Gently said: 'From the beginning, your wife and you have taken opposite sides. She wants to keep us pointed towards Pederson and you want to absolve him from suspicion. Yet you were there. You have vital information. Perhaps information that would help us close this case. Why do you still seek to keep it from us, and are even willing to tell tales on your wife?'

'That . . . wasn't a tale!'

'But you needn't have told it.'

'Yes, you had to know why—!'

Gently shook his head. 'Your wife was perhaps guilty of a little deception, but I feel convinced that her account of the matter is the truth. You spoke of those things to her, and she and your neighbour are prepared to give statements.'

'But if I deny them?'

'Still the question is why.'

'Because—because!'

'Yes?'

Herbert Bacon bowed his head. He said: 'It isn't enough, what I know. Not enough to put him away. If I told you everything it wouldn't help, just make it awkward for the poor bloke.' He gave a little shudder. 'He may have done it,' he said. 'I'm not saying that everything isn't against him. But that was back then, a lifetime

181

ago, and I don't think it's fair to carry on blaming him. Cissy does, but I'm not Cissy. I'd soonest we forgot the whole affair.'

It could have been Sir Tommy sitting there in the greenhouse!

'You have no regard, then, for the girl you once knew?'

'Yes . . . if it had happened last week! But not now, all this time afterwards.'

'A young girl in the bloom of youth?'

'I know, I know! But it's too long ago.'

Gently studied the averted face. 'Then let's put it this way,' he said. 'There may never be an arrest in this case, but at least we should make an effort to come by the truth. Suspicion doesn't wholly rest with Pederson, and furthermore your evidence could be of service to him.'

Now his face did turn. 'You mean—?'

'I mean it were best we get at the truth.'

The watery eyes gazed long, but at last drifted back to the row of pots.

'I . . . saw him.'

'You can vouch that it was Pederson.'

He nodded. 'Yes. It's like I told Cissy. He'd just come out from the men's toilets, and he was lighting a cheroot.'

'Did he see you?'

'No, I shouldn't think so. He was looking towards the mess. I had a light on in the other side, but the black-out was good and it didn't show.'

'Did you know that Miss Read was at the dance?'

'I didn't know for certain, but it wasn't likely she would have missed it.'

'Did you know of her intentions that night?'

'Cissy knew. Nobody told me.'

'Can you estimate the time when Pederson came out?'

'I think they had a dance still to go. You could hear the band plainly in the toilets, and they struck up again soon after he left.'

'Left—in which direction?'

'Round the back of the mess, the way you'd go towards the hut. I saw him pass that window, as I told you, and then his footsteps died away.'

'Weren't you curious about what he was up to—out there on his own, on a cold night?'

'Perhaps—a bit. But he could just have been going that way back to the mess. It wasn't any further.'

'It didn't occur to you to follow him?'

'No, why would it? I still had a job to get done.'

'So that's the long and the short of your testimony.'

'I told you it wasn't going to help you.'

Gently sighed. 'So, after all, there wasn't much need for you to hold out on us, and I take it that now you will be willing to provide a signed statement.'

He hesitated. 'Do I have to?'

Gently nodded. 'We shall be in touch. Will this evening be convenient?'

He gazed at the pots. 'I suppose so.'

'Then that's all for now, Mr Bacon. I'll leave you to get on with whatever I interrupted.'

He rose. Herbert Bacon remained sitting, a forlorn figure among his plants. As Gently passed the bungalow the cat stretched itself lazily, but there was no longer a face peering through the window . . .

CHAPTER TEN

'Well . . . I don't know, sir. I can't think Sir Tommy would be too pleased.'

Tea was on the table when Gently got back to Heatherings but his first move was towards the phone. At the table, Gabrielle waited impatiently, and Mrs Jarvis hovered by the door, but to no purpose. With barely a glance at them he had picked up the phone and stabbed in a number.

Sir Tommy or no, hadn't the time come to indulge in a little unorthodox action? It was a case beyond the usual run of inquiries, a ctime obscured in a veil of years. The very location had been swept away except for that mouldering hut among the trees: there remained no evidence and no clues: merely memories, obstructions and lies.

'I want you to summon those three people to the police station. There is every reason to fetch them in. Bacon is now prepared to give a statement and the other two have additions to make to theirs.'

'But to have them in together, sir!'

'You can lay the blame on me.'

'Don't you think we ought to clear it—'

'I'll be with you at the station at seven.'

He hung up, shrugging. Would it buy them anything? Perhaps and perhaps not: but it was worth a try! However long the odds against it leading to a positive result . . .

Half in a dream, he took his place at the table and accepted the cup of tea that Mrs Jarvis had poured for him.

'That was Eyke you were ringing . . . ?'

'Yes. I shall be going into town after tea.'

'You have learned something from that lady's husband?'

'A very little. But now he's ready to admit to it.'

Gabrielle nodded, but pressed him no further: she had learned to understand Gently's moods. Silently they ate their meal, with an occasional interruption from Mrs Jarvis. Outside, the sun was going down in full glory, lighting a distant skein of cloud.

'You will not be late?'

'Probably not. But don't wait up for me if I am.'

He drove into town early and went to drink

185

a half in The Pelican. It was early season and the bar nearly empty, just a couple of the regulars discussing football. From the window he watched the street, where the traffic also was scant; and saw at last a patrol-car passing, a patrol-car with passengers in the rear seat.

'Fill you up?'

He shook his head. Another patrol-car was passing. He paused a little longer, to fill his pipe; then continued on his way to the police station.

*   *   *

'Where have you put them?'

Herbert Bacon was sitting alone on a bench in reception. He looked round nervously as Gently entered, and seemed as though he were about to say something.

'In my office. Potty's with them. They weren't too happy about coming here.'

'I want the three of them together.'

'I know that's what you said, sir. But I thought it best . . .'

'Bring Bacon along.'

Eyke shook his head, but signalled to the nervous Bacon. The latter rose reluctantly and was ushered ahead of them down the passage that led to Eyke's office. Did he suspect something? It seemed not unlikely, though he had arrived there after the two Americans. At the door of the office he hesitated, sent an

186

appealing look towards Gently.

'I thought I was here to—'

'Just go through.'

'But—'

Eyke opened the door and thrust Bacon inside.

It wasn't a big office, and there weren't enough chairs. Two were already occupied by Pederson and Osborne. They were sitting apart, one at either end of the desk, one with his back half-turned to the other. Potton was standing uncomfortably by the door and seemed relieved to see the others enter.

'Fetch a couple more chairs, Potty.'

For a long moment there was silence in the office. Pederson was staring at nothing, Osborne at the shrinking figure of Bacon. It was Osborne who spoke: he fixed an angry eye on Gently.

'Fella, you better tell us what the game is,' he said. 'We're not just here to add bits to our statements, you've got something else in mind.'

'Perhaps a little more than that.'

'Yeah, I can see. And who is that guy you've got over there?'

'In a moment I shall be introducing him.'

'You don't have to tell me—I think I can guess.'

Potton lugged the chairs in and set them out. Eyke signalled that Gently should take the chair behind the desk. Instead, he requested

187

Potton to bring it round the desk and place it along with the others. Osborne watched the arrangement with a curious look.

'So we're just going to chew the rag?' he said. 'Nobody gets jumped on?'

'A discussion,' Gently said. 'Between the three people who have the most to tell us.'

Osborne's eyes narrowed. 'The three people,' he said. 'Then that guy is the fellow I think he is.'

'Mr Herbert Bacon, a retired builder,' Gently said.

'Surest thing,' Osborne said. 'Surest thing.' He slid a look towards Pederson, who ignored it.

'So, if we can all be seated.'

Behind them, Potton closed the door. The hapless Bacon chose a seat as far from the other two as he could get. Gently advanced to the desk to knock out his pipe, then retired to his chair, placed nearest the door. He made himself comfortable, put away the pipe, let his eye stray to the Americans and Bacon.

'Perhaps you will begin, Mr Bacon,' he said. 'A brief account of your business at the camp that night. What you were doing, where you were, and the approximate time you were present there.'

'Oh . . . but please!'

'You have nothing to fear. A simple resumé of the facts.'

'But . . . I mean!'

188

'At the time, I believe, you were engaged by the builder responsible for the camp.'

Wretchedly, Bacon fumbled with his hands, tried to keep his faltering gaze away from the Americans. Osborne's eyes were fixing him: Pederson was still staring into space.

'Stringer. . . that's what his name was.'

'The name of the builder who employed you.'

'Yes. It was him who built the camp . . . then afterwards he looked after the maintenance.'

'So you were often around there.'

'Yes . . .'

'You would know by sight some of the servicemen stationed there.'

'Well . . .'

'Wasn't that the case?'

'Yes! I mean, I knew a few of them.'

Gently nodded. 'So let's come to that day, the thirty-first of January, nineteen forty-four. Presumably you were working on the camp that day, and were persuaded to put in some overtime.'

'Yes . . . overtime.'

'Could you be specific?'

'I . . . the foreman asked me if I could stay! There was a job we'd been putting off, and someone had got on to him about it.'

'What was the job?'

'It wasn't important . . .'

'A job you could handle by yourself, was it?'

The calloused hands were struggling. 'Yes.'

'Like—adding some fitments to the toilets?'

Now Pederson's eyes were suddenly alert!

'Go on,' Gently said. 'Tell me about it.'

'I—I'd sooner . . . !'

'Tell me.'

For a moment it seemed that Bacon might be going to dry up.

'Well?'

'It was just a mirror—a mirror and a shelf! I'd got the wood, and the mirror was waiting there. I wasn't going to paint it, not then.'

'And that was the work that occupied you that evening?'

All he could manage was a nod.

'And the toilets would have been where?'

In a mumble he spoke it: 'Behind the officer's mess.'

*   *   *

'That bonzo is lying!'

As though he'd been stung, Pederson jolted upright in his chair, his fleshy features flushed, his brown eyes boring at the wilting Bacon. Osborne was also staring, but in his case it was at Pederson.

'If you don't mind, Mr Pederson . . .'

'But that bastard is telling you a tale! He was never in the toilets that night, wherever else he may have been.'

'Shall we hear him out?'

'He's telling lies!'

190

'Still, if we can just hear what he has to say.'

'Listen schmuck, I was in that toilets, and there was no other bastard there but me.'

'In . . . either side of the toilets?'

'Whaddya mean?'

'I'm told there were sides for both women and men.'

'And you're telling me this louse—?'

'I think you'll find that the toilets Mr Bacon was working in was the ladies.'

Pederson's stare was widening. 'But I must have seen the guy—or heard him!'

'Not necessarily. The band was playing in the mess, and the two toilets would no doubt have been well separated.'

'They were concrete-built,' Osborne put in. 'I guess you'd do well to lay off, Kit. If the guy says he was there he was there, whether somebody likes it or not.'

'You mean I just got to take it?'

'Might be best.'

Pederson glared at him, but bit his lip.

'So,' Gently said. 'If we can get on. I believe the job took you all the evening, Mr Bacon. You were there from some time after tea till after you heard the band stop playing.'

Bacon was trembling. 'Please . . .'

'Just continue your account, Mr Bacon.'

'But . . . really!'

'If you will.'

He stared down at his clasped hands.

'For example, would you have had your

191

meal at the camp?'

'I—yes . . . they let us use the airmen's mess. Then I fetched my gear from the compound . . . it would have been about seven. The band started up later.'

'You found the toilets empty?'

He nodded. 'I used the gent's side . . . there wasn't anyone in there then. Then I went round to the other side and got on with making up the shelf.'

'You had your tool-box with you?'

'No—I mean! I kept my tool-box strapped to my bike . . . I just took in the tools I needed. I had to leave my bike outside . . .'

'Go on.'

He seemed almost unable to, aware of the hostile eyes trained on him. After several hesitations he blurted:

'My plane . . . I needed my plane.'

'You had finished making the shelf?'

He nodded. 'I'd cut out the pieces, but they needed a trim . . .'

'Can you remember when it was?'

'No . . . later on!'

'Towards the end of the dancing?'

He didn't reply.

'So . . . you went outside to fetch your plane. Didn't you see something while you were out there?'

'I . . .'

'Well?'

'I saw—someone!'

192

'Someone?'

His head sank even lower. 'A man. He'd come out of the other toilet. He . . . was lighting a cheroot, so I saw his face . . .'

'A face you recognised?'

He managed a nod.

'Someone here present?'

He stared at his lap.

'Oh, come out with it, fella!' Osborne interrupted. 'We know goddamn well who was in that toilet. Kit here went out to cool off for a spell. If you saw anyone, you saw him.'

'Lay off!' Pederson snarled. 'You'd do best to.'

Osborne stared at him, his eyes narrowing.

'Was it former First Lieutenant Pederson you saw?' Gently said.

'I . . .'

'Was it?'

The ghost of a nod. 'He lit a cheroot. And then . . .'

'And then . . . ?'

'He went off round the end of the mess.'

'Liar!' Pederson had started up from his chair, seemed ready to pounce on the fearful Bacon. Potton moved hastily from covering the door to be in a position to step between them.

'Please sit down, Mr Pederson.'

'That slob never saw me—!'

'Please be good enough to control yourself.'

'But if you're going to believe him—!'

'If you will just sit down.'

193

Pederson gave a snarl, but threw himself back on his chair. He stared murderously at Bacon, his hands gripped into fists.

Osborne, meanwhile, had never taken his eyes off Pederson.

Gently said: 'Then you wish to deny having left the toilet, Mr Pederson?'

'Deny it—yeah, of course I deny it! I stuck around in there till the band packed in, you got all that in my statement.'

'You didn't once step outside?'

'No, I never did—!'

'Not to light a cheroot?'

'Oh hell! I may have done. As I recall, that toilet was niffy, I could have stepped out for a breath of air.'

'Then Mr Bacon may well have seen you.'

'Yeah—but I'm saying that's all he saw! Me stepping out for some pure air, and maybe lighting up while I was out there.'

'He couldn't have seen you leave in the direction mentioned.'

'No, he goddamn couldn't.'

'Or passing by a lit window at the end of the mess.'

'What sodding lit window? There was a black-out.'

Gently said: 'When you left the mess it was to avoid a situation that was painful to you. How it would end you were fairly certain, but you were still not entirely positive.'

Pederson glared. 'Whaddya getting at,

194

fella?'

Gently said: 'You were advised of the time when that situation would conclude. While you were waiting out there in the toilet, may you not have felt an urge to seek confirmation?'

An exclamation from Osborne! Pederson kept glaring.

'Are you saying I went round to peek at them, fella?'

Gently shrugged. 'Would that have been unlikely—when there is testimony that seems to bear it out?'

'Testimony my arse!'

'You admit you left the toilet.'

'Yeah, yeah, to light me a cheroot. But then I went straight back in, and never showed my nose again till the dance was over.' He glowered at Bacon. 'So who says different? Who's going to let on that I'm telling a lie?'

Not Bacon, that was apparent! The retired builder didn't dare lift his head. It was Osborne who picked up the challenge, his eyes fixed tightly on the sweating Pederson.

'Kit—I've got to come in on this. It's me who is going to call you a liar . . .'

'Don't you dare!'

'I've got to, Kit. I know, you know, that you were out there.'

'Chuck, I'm warning you.'

'I'm sorry, Kit. But it all squares with what I remember. We heard someone, Milly and me, down towards the far end of the mess-hall. I guessed it was you, but now I know—I could see the red end of your cheroot.'

'You saw—nothing!'

'Yes. It was because of it that Milly broke us up. She shoved me back into the mess and took off to collect her bike.' Osborne paused, his stare even tighter. 'And that left you alone out there with Milly. Just you and her. The next day I meant to speak to you about it, but you know what happened that day.'

Sweat was standing out on Pederson's brow. 'You, you're asking for it, Chuck!' he said. 'Next thing I was tucking her under the concrete—is that what you want this guy to believe?'

'I'm saying you were out there with her.'

'Yeah—and I'm saying you'd better lay off!'

'You and she. Alone.'

'Only . . . it wasn't like that, fella. Was it?'

Osborne said nothing. Pederson dashed at the sweat. His staring eyes turned on Gently. 'Fella,' he said. 'I wasn't going to say this, but like I ain't being left with the choice.' He flicked more sweat. 'Yeah,' he said. 'I did go round there. Like you said, I couldn't leave it alone. I had to know. I hung on in that goddamn toilet till I couldn't take it any longer. I came out a couple of times, and that guy sitting there could have seen me. But it got close to the time when I knew she'd be leaving, and that was it, I slunk off round.'

Gently nodded. 'You took up a position

196

where you had the door of the mess-hall in view?'

'Nope, I hung back, they were already out there, I sure as hell didn't want to get too close. I couldn't see them, fella, but I could hear them, and that was enough to turn my stomach.' He threw a look at the glowering Osborne. 'I guess they must have heard me too,' he said. 'I must have stepped on something, and they went quiet for a moment, then they were arguing, but keeping it down.'

He broke off, his lips taut.

'And then?'

He scuffed at his brow. 'I guess I have to tell you! They went quiet for a bit, but then I heard them again, further off, down towards the hut.'

'Towards . . . the hut?'

'Yeah. And I heard them open the door. And that's it, fella, I blew, I couldn't bear to think what they were at in there, I just took off like crazy, back round the mess, towards the airfield. But when I got back to the mess Chuck was in there ahead of me, so I was guessing he couldn't have got very far with her.'

'You louse, Kit—you louse!'

Now they were both of them on their feet, the bushy-haired Osborne, the flush-faced Pederson, facing each other with flaming eyes. In his chair, the frightened Bacon was cringeing as far from them as he could get.

'Chuck, I had to tell him—I warned you to lay off!'

'You had that tale made all ready!'

'Only it isn't a tale!'

'A goddamn tale. Milly never would let me go with her to the hut!'

'Chuck, I heard you—'

'You heard nothing. And Robbo knows when I went back in. There was only one guy left out there with Milly, and you know who that guy was.'

'I heard you open the door—'

'Forget it!'

'It's true—I didn't make it up!'

'Just ask this guy here if he's believing you—and he's an expert when it comes to tales.'

Pederson swung round to face Gently, but Gently met him with his blankest stare.

'You see, it isn't going to wash,' Osborne sneered. 'And now you've got him wondering why you ever came up with it—a guy with opportunity and a motive like yours. You want to tell him?'

'But you know it's true, Chuck!'

'Sure, sure. But he only has to ask Robbo.'

'You were outside long enough—'

'But motive I didn't have.'

'It's my word against yours!'

'So try to make it stick, Bud.'

Time to call a halt . . .? They had each moved a step closer, Pederson with fists still clenched. He was shorter than Osborne, who had drawn himself up and was staring down at the other with challenging eyes. Which did one believe? Two tales . . . had the balance a little tilted between the pair? Gently rose also.

'Thank you, gentlemen,' he said. 'You have each added something to our knowledge of this affair. Perhaps what we can usefully do now is to pass on to completing your statements. You are prepared to do this?'

Osborne's shoulders twitched. 'I am! I can't answer for other guys.'

Pederson's glare was dangerous. 'You get mine the way I told it!' he snarled.

'In that case we can proceed. The Chief Inspector here will make the arrangements. Mr Bacon may stay in the office and write his statement at the desk.'

Eyke had risen at the same time as Gently. He fumbled in the desk for a statement-form and laid it out, ready for Bacon. Then he signalled to Potton, who opened the door, and requested the two Americans to follow him.

'Take this chair, Mr Bacon.'

Gently lit his pipe, and retired to a seat near the window. Again, it was the same question! Had they really got any further?

He smoked, watched the setting sun, heard the nervous rustlings of the pen behind him. Sometimes it paused for long moments before setting off again in quick bursts . . .

A knock on the door: it opened to reveal Eyke's sergeant, Campsey.

'Sir, if you could spare a moment! That relative of the victim's has just turned up and wants to have a word with someone. The Chief Inspector has got his hands full, so I was wondering if you wouldn't mind . . .'

'You stay here.'

'Yes, of course, sir!'

In reception sat a lonely figure: a man close to his eighties, who rose with difficulty and held out a quivering hand to Gently.

'Forgive me for being late . . . the traffic . . .'

He was dressed in a smartly-cut grey suit with, on the chair beside him, a matching trilby and pair of gloves. The brother . . . His features, though ageing, suggested a distinction, a strength of personality.

'I suppose . . . there's no doubt?'

Gently shook his head.

'Of course, we always knew that something like this . . . But it's still a shock, after all this time. I still find it difficult to believe.'

'You were close to your sister?'

'Yes. She was younger than me by a few years. I could never understand why she chose the Land Army, but there it was, she wanted to try something different.'

'She kept in touch with you?'

He nodded. 'That's what made it so unbelievable. Everything was arranged, it was to be in June, so why would she suddenly throw it all up? I was to be her best man.'

'Her—best man?'

'Yes.'

'Then . . . you knew your sister had become engaged?'

'Of course.'

'And you had known for some time?'

'Yes. We'd known since the summer of the previous year.'

'Since the summer . . .'

'I thought you would know about it. Her letters were full of it at the time. She was going to marry the son of the farmer she worked for—Bacon his name was. Herbert Bacon.'

'Herbert . . . Bacon.'

'We'd never met him, of course. He was going to pay us a visit that Easter. But then . . . well, you know what happened. I wrote him a letter, but he didn't reply.'

Very slowly, Gently nodded.

'There—won't be any problems, will there?' Read said. 'I'm her only living relative, but I know our parents would have wanted it. We've a family plot in the churchyard at home.'

'There won't be any problems,' Gently said.

*　　　*　　　*

'Fetch them back to the office.'

'But sir—they're in the middle of making their statements!'

'So they can finish them later on. At the moment, I want them back in the office.'

'But—!'

'Just fetch them.'

Bacon, at least, had finished his statement. Gently picked it up and glanced through it—no possible doubt: he could swear to Pederson.

'So—what game are we on now?'

Osborne came in looking wary, Pederson with a defiant scowl. They stood uncertainly in the middle of the office, while Potton closed the door again behind them.

'Be seated, gentlemen.'

'But I don't get it—!'

Bacon had already resumed his chair. Growling, Osborne took his, and Pederson, after a moment, dumped himself opposite. Gently remained standing.

'Now, gentlemen,' he said. 'I've just had an interesting conversation with a man called Read. The victim's brother.'

'Milly had a brother . . . ?'

'An affectionate brother. One with whom she was in regular communication. Who she had elected to be best man at her wedding in the June of the year when she died.'

'But . . . fella! That can't have been possible!'

'Quite possible,' Gently said.

'She never would have had the chance to tell him!'

'Every chance. The engagement took place in the preceding summer.'

'The summer! But we never came here—'

Gently nodded. 'Not you,' he said.

202

'You mean—she had another?'

'She had another.'

'Then who the hell—!'

'Someone here can answer that.'

'Oh . . . my God!'

Osborne's eye flew to Bacon: Pederson's glare fastened on him too. The trembling retired builder raised a calloused hand, as though to ward off a blow.

'But that was before . . .!'

'You louse—you were engaged to her?'

'I tell you . . . please!'

'You got a wedding fixed too?'

'It was before . . .'

'And that night you hung around there—cooked up some job so you could keep an eye on her?'

'No—please! It was all over then . . .'

'Yeah,' Osborne said. 'And it's all over now! You were the rat who went into that hut with her—the rat who Kit heard talking to her.'

'I was in the toilets . . . I didn't . . .'

'You killed Milly!'

'No!'

'You did. She told you she was through with you, and you couldn't take it. And that's how she finished up under the concrete!'

'Please . . . you've got to listen!'

'Do I have to shake it out of you?'

'Stop him!' Gently exclaimed, but Osborne had already plucked Bacon from his chair, was shaking the retired builder like a dog shaking a rat. Potton grappled with him, hauled him away. Bacon collapsed on the floor. Something had fallen from his pocket, a cigarette case of tarnished silver. Osborne saw it, gave a cry, wrenched himself from Potton's grasp. He snatched the case up, turned it over to reveal initials engraved upon it.

'My case! The one I gave Milly for a token on that night . . .'

'You gave it to Miss Read?'

'I gave it to Milly. Now ask that snake how he came by it!'

Bacon was hauling himself up from the floor. He seemed unable to understand. He sank back on his chair, sobbing, his face buried in his hands.

'Yeah,' Osborne said. 'Yeah. So now we know, Kit. Now we know.'

CHAPTER ELEVEN

'It all happened so long ago . . .'

Hadn't that been the signature tune from the beginning? They were dealing with ghosts: it was only the victim who was resisting the floods of time. Millicent Read could never grow old. Her remains stayed those of a young girl. She had taken her departure from time and could never now be dragged back into it.

All else had been swept on, from decade

to decade, from youth to age. Memories remained, souvenirs, record, but never could return that moment of time.

'My memory . . . I sometimes think . . .'

Lights had been switched on in the office. The two Americans, their statements completed, had been dispatched back to their guest-house.

'A drop of something . . . ?'

Bacon was sitting with an empty glass at his elbow. You couldn't get his eye. He was gazing bemusedly, his roughened hands lying slackly in his lap.

'I suppose . . .'

'You must have known that she had changed?'

'Yes, I noticed . . . But I trusted Milly!'

'When she grew so fond of attending those dances?'

'Yes, but she told me . . .'

'That she just enjoyed the dancing?'

On the desk a tape recorder was relentlessly turning while, in addition, a W.P.C. was scribbling notes on a pad. Beside Gently Eyke sat staring, sometimes at Bacon, sometimes at the desk, and Metfield had been appointed to guard the door.

'But, in the end, you must have had your suspicions. That job in the toilets—was it really so urgent?'

'No . . . I volunteered for it. It was something I heard her telling Cissy.'

'You volunteered for it?'

'Yes. I felt I should . . . I had to know! The toilets were near the mess-hall, and I thought, if I kept my eye open . . .'

'You went out frequently?'

'No. I knew I wouldn't see her till the dancing was over. So I got the job done as soon as I could, and then went out there . . . over by the trees.'

'This would have been after you'd seen Pederson.'

'Yes . . . it's true, he did go back in. It must have been later . . .'

'And you waited under the trees?'

'A car or something could have come, she might have seen me.'

'How long were you waiting there?'

'I can't remember . . .'

'But you saw them come out. Miss Read and Osborne.'

'I . . . saw them.' His gaze never faltered. 'Him and her. They showed up, coming out . . . they had to push through the black-out curtains. Then it was dark again. But I was close enough to hear . . .'

'You heard him propose to her.'

He was silent.

'You did hear him, Mr Bacon?'

Still he said nothing.

'Would you tell us, please?'

At last, a mutter from him! 'Yes . . .'

'Thank you, Mr Bacon. And—you heard

her acceptance?'

Another long pause! 'Yes . . .'

Gently nodded. 'Miss Read accepted him, and there followed a demonstration of affection between them. This was interrupted by something they heard, apparently a sound made by Pederson. Were you aware of his presence there?'

'I . . . no.'

'But you were a witness to the couple parting.'

'He—he wanted to go to the hut with her, but she wouldn't have it. She made him go inside.'

'You saw him go in.'

'Yes . . .'

'And—Miss Read?'

Was he going to dry up? For the first time the hands moved, very slowly, as though merely seeking a more comfortable position.

Gently said: 'We have Pederson's testimony that he heard Miss Read in conversation with a man near the hut. It could not have been Osborne, who you saw re-enter the mess. Could it credibly have been some person other than yourself?'

Silence: the hands motionless.

'Well?'

Not the flicker of a lid.

'Would you answer the question?'

Nothing.

And then he burst into hysterical tears.

207

'I can't believe it—I can't! It was something that happened to somebody else!' He was howling, weaving in the chair, dashing at the tears running down his creased cheeks. 'I loved her, it wasn't possible, I could never believe it was me who did it—it wasn't me, something happened in there, but I swear it wasn't me!'

The W.P.C. was staring in alarm, her pencil unable to scribble. Eyke was gazing at Bacon, sitting bolt-upright. Metfield had taken an uncertain step forward. And Gently was silent.

'I told her—I told her—I wanted her happy! I'd have let her go with him if that's what she wanted. But she was trying to be kind, so kind, and I couldn't bear it. I couldn't bear it! She was too good to me—too good. I couldn't let it go on! And it happened, something happened. The next thing . . . the next thing . . .'

He covered his face and howled.

'I didn't know—I've never known! It was like I was watching someone else, someone strange who I didn't know. It's never been me. All these years I could never believe it was me. I couldn't have done it, it wasn't possible, it was a dream I'd had, a bad dream. I married Cissy, I was Cissy's husband. Cissy's husband was who I was . . . And she was just there, under the concrete, nothing, nothing, a bad dream!' He howled. 'Can't you understand—

please, please! Say you understand!'

Gently stared at him, but said nothing. Fresh tears gushed from the rheumy eyes.

'The concrete,' he said. 'The concrete. It was bust when they dumped a dud engine there. I only had to lift the bits and put them back over again. The engine had made a hollow, so it finished up flat. And there was a dump of discarded engine-covers in the corner, I only had to pull them over . . .'

Gently said: 'Two were found with the body.'

'I know, I know!'

'And her bicycle had to be disposed of.'

'I threw it in the pond.'

'She would have had a handbag.'

'I threw that in the pond too!'

'But—not the cigarette case.'

'I—no!' He dashed at the tears. 'I found it on the floor after . . . after . . .'

'After your disposal of the body had been completed.'

'Yes. I must have shoved it in my pocket. I only found it later on, in my bedroom at the farm. I stuffed it away somewhere . . . it was years later . . .'

'Look at me, Bacon.'

'Please—no!'

'Look at me.'

'Please!'

'Bacon, I want you to tell me in so many words that it was you who killed Millicent

209

Read.'

'I . . . I . . . !'

'In so many words.'

Desperately, he jerked his face away.

'Bacon.'

'I—I killed Milly!'

And the tape recorder kept turning.

*   *   *

'When he's signed his statement, drive him home.'

'But I can't, sir!'

'I think you may.'

An hour later they were sitting alone in the office with mugs of coffee, Gently with his pipe going. In the interrogation room next-door a typewriter was fretting away, occasionally varied by the sound of voices as a query was raised and answered. In the office there had been mainly silence as both men sat digesting the situation. Now Eyke was looking aghast.

'But Sir Tommy, sir—I couldn't!'

'I'll give him a ring when I get back'

'But chummie is due before the beak tomorrow . . .'

'I don't think Bacon is going to run away.'

'I don't know, sir . . .'

'I will take responsibility.'

Eyke shook his head doubtfully and stared at the blotter on his desk.

'It isn't an everyday case,' Gently said.

'All the same, sir!'

Gently puffed.

Perhaps the only question still remaining was the degree of implication of Cissy Bacon—had she been aware of her husband's guilt when trying so hard to direct them towards Pederson? Suspicion she must have had. All the facts were known to her, of Herbert Bacon's situation with regard to the victim, of the probability of the latter's defection, of Bacon's presence on the night of the disappearance. Perhaps . . . even then? But certainly after the discovery of the concealed remains! Then suspicion had turned to fear, and the first anonymous note had been sent . . . Worth pursuing? He shrugged. Even in the case of her wretched husband . . .

'I'll leave it with you.'

'Don't think I'm not grateful, sir, but . . .'

'We don't need to lock him in a cell.'

'Well, if you really think . . .'

When he arrived back at Welbourne The Bell was still open, and he paused there for a quick half. Sid was curious, and welcomed him eagerly, but Gently was in no mood to relay information.

'You are late, my dear . . .'

The same at Heatherings. There, Sir Tommy kept him on the phone for half an hour, at first was unable to believe what he was hearing, and then to tender congratulations enough.

211

'I'll ring that damned Major—what's his name? Him and his blasted threats! But you're dead sure we've got a case, George—no chance of this fellow squirming out?'

'Confession, testimony and evidence.'

'Well, it's a weight off my mind!'

Gabrielle, of course, had been listening, but wanted the details over again.

'I do not know,' she said at last. 'But is it fair that you put this poor old man on trial? It is how many years? Too many! Is it not enough that we should know?'

'There is a chance that the courts may agree with you.'

Gabrielle nodded. 'So we wait and see! He has perhaps received punishment enough by becoming married to that dreadful lady.'

And perhaps he had . . .

'Let's go to bed.'

'Aha.'

By then, the dreadful lady and her husband should have been reunited.

*   *   *

Major Forrest called. Sir Tommy. The brother of the deceased had no wish for them to press charges. Nevertheless the case proceeded, though reduced from one of murder to one of unlawful killing. The trial was set for the following August and meanwhile Bacon was released on bail, a sale notice appeared at the bungalow, and neither he nor his wife were seen again in the village. But . . . was it still any more than a farce? In the end it was Mrs Jarvis who brought the news to Heatherings. Just a fortnight before the trial was due to commence, a Queen's Pardon had been awarded to Herbert Reginald Bacon . . .

'It's because of when it happened, Mr Gently . . .'

Yes. When the Yanks were Over Here.

And, some time later, the Nissen hut was dismantled, to allow brambles to creep over broken concrete.

Brundall, 1997

We hope you have enjoyed this Large
Print book. Other Chivers Press or
Thorndike Press Large Print books are
available at your library or directly from the
publishers.

For more information about current and
forthcoming titles, please call or write,
without obligation, to:

Chivers Large Print
published by BBC Audiobooks Ltd
St James House, The Square
Lower Bristol Road
Bath BA2 3SB
UK
email: bbcaudiobooks@bbc.co.uk
www.bbcaudiobooks.co.uk

OR

Thorndike Press
295 Kennedy Memorial Drive,
Waterville
Maine 04901
USA
www.gale.com/thorndike
www.gale.com/wheeler

All our Large Print titles are designed for
easy reading, and all our books are made to
last.